Book Two: Battle for Shady Oaks

Char Robinson

There are so many people to thank and I would love to dedicate this novel to them all. I do want to thank my parents for buying me books and allowing me to spend hours reading them.

For the purposes of this book, one person stands out. I'd like to dedicate this novel to my Aunt Kay. Thank you for reading to me when I was small. Thank you for all those scary stories, and yes — you almost had me convinced you were a vampire. Almost.

Chapter One

Charlie was met by Candice Vaughn as he sauntered through the door to the Mayor's office. She vigorously waved a piece of paper in the air.

"Glad you're here, I came in and Dave's Place has been trying to get hold of us since yesterday morning. I took this message from Lilly."

She handed the paper to him and folded her arms over her ample bosom. Candice was in her late sixties, but she hustled and bustled everywhere as though she were much younger. Her bright blue eyes were shining behind her granny glasses; gray curls bobbed and danced around her cherubic face.

"They were about ready to send a team over here to check on us, good thing I came by to bring your supper!"

Charlie fondly patted her shoulder as he scanned the message. Candice was one of the first survivors they found over in Harris and everyone was glad she was around. She quickly became the one everyone went to when they needed advice or a friendly ear.

"They want a progress report and also want to know if it's

possible to send more people this way."

Charlie rubbed his chin thoughtfully and said, "I'm surprised that they're still getting so many survivors out of the city, they've had ten in the last week. Guess it's getting crowded over there."

When the zombie infection was in its beginning stages, he stumbled upon Hudson Place where Dave Martin and his wife, Lilly, took him in. There were other families sheltering inside the huge warehouse as well, and they helped him get to Shady Oaks to find his daughter. After Dave was murdered by the Connor Group, they renamed the warehouse Dave's Place and it now served as a way station for survivors from Ambrose.

Candice nodded. "Well we certainly have the room for them now; two-thirds of the houses here are still empty, although they're clean and ready for new folks."

Charlie remembered when Shady Oaks had been a mess. They hunted down and destroyed all the undead and rescued the survivors, which included his daughter, Jenny and her fiancé, Jake.

They then spent the next few weeks cleaning homes and businesses, making lists of what was available in the way of goods, and getting everything running. The water plant was operational as well as several wind turbines and windmills, which reduced their need for generators. Air conditioning was still unavailable except in the court house building. The system was still too fragile, but with each day warmer than the next, they had to cool at least one building so anyone who needed to could find some relief.

He'd seen a few of the teens already swimming in the park's small lake and let it slide because they took off when they saw him. Being the newly elected Mayor still didn't feel quite right, and he decided that a little illegal swimming was one battle he didn't think was worth fighting at the time. If it became a problem he'd have a little talk with their parents later.

Most of the nearby farms were fine, the hardy people who lived there managed to take care of any zombie that wandered onto their property. There was one dairy and three other farms provided hay, wheat, and corn. Another farm provided most of their meat and was stocked with pigs, goats, beef cattle, and chickens. Most of the occupied homes in town were growing their own plots of fresh vegetables, training courtesy of Candice and a few others.

Although spring was rolling into summer and it was still early, everyone decided it wasn't too soon to plan for winter. Each occupied home was fitted to burn wood in the winter and two teams went out almost every day to chop and gather wood. If more people were being sent to Shady Oaks, that meant more helping hands, and Charlie was all for that.

"Candice, would you send them a reply and let them know we'd be glad to have them come on down here. Reggie is up there – he and a friend of his brought them some fresh produce and a few other supplies. He could bring some of them back with him when he returns tomorrow. We can use all the help we can get right now."

She beamed and nodded her head vigorously. "Be glad to! Don't worry your head about it one little bit, I'll do it right now."

As she bustled off, humming to herself, Charlie grinned at her retreating figure before turning and heading for his office. As soon as he walked through the doorway, he saw the tray covered with a tea towel on top of his desk. He walked over and peeked underneath. Fried chicken, mashed potatoes, green beans, and salad greeted him. A large glass of sweet tea that was beginning to sweat sat next to the tray.

Usually Judith sent him off with a hefty lunch, but she was busy helping Jake and Jenny with another project. As he sat down and dug into the chicken, he groaned with delight. Candice was one of the best cooks in town and she knew it. He often teased her that if she were a few years younger she wouldn't be able to beat him off with a stick, which made her giggle like a school girl.

She was filling in for Rose at the station and he enjoyed her company. Rose and Dexter took a few days off to spend time with their son, Kevin. Families were being encouraged to spend some time relaxing with family or friends, and it was their turn. Most stayed home or went fishing at the park's lake or on one of the farm ponds; no one wanted to stray too far from town. Charlie met the Reed's at Dave's Place and although everyone found Dexter brutish and offensive at times, Rose and Kevin were highly regarded by all, and they were

7

happily settled into a new home in Shady Oaks.

Other activities were slowly coming back, a baseball game was scheduled for the following Saturday, and Charlie was sure the entire town would be there. Jake, the town's young doctor, suggested the days off and bringing back community events because people were on the verge of mental collapse after losing so many of their family and friends. Some even suffered with the memory of having to destroy someone they knew and cared about.

So far his plan seemed to be working, more people had smiles on their faces and the town was beginning to run more efficiently. They were all adjusting to the new normal of their lives, and Charlie was glad to see hope and optimism slowly returning.

Charlie finished his meal and as he cut the first piece of cherry cobbler and lifted it to his mouth, Travis, Judith's son, burst through the door and skidded to a stop in front of the desk.

He pointed toward the outer doors. He was panting and Charlie waited for him to catch his breath.

"Mom sent me," he gasped out. He placed both hands on the edge anything to be able to live like this again."

They all nodded. "I'm hoping someday we can go back to Ambrose and see about helping the people still trapped there," Brooke said softly.

She looked up at the adults. "I feel strongly about that, even though I don't talk about it much," she shook her head. "I can't stop thinking about how much we have now and how there are people out there barely surviving and probably dying."

"I never knew you felt that way," Cindy said as she put her arm around her daughter to give her a hug. "Let's talk more about this later, okay?" At Brooke's nod, she smiled and stood, pulling Brooke up with her and giving her another quick hug.

The men all stood and Mick motioned toward the door. "Guess it's time we all head on over and find out what's going on."

As they trudged through the grass still damp with late morning dew, Mick and Charlie both had the same thought. Please let this not be about the Connor Group. Neither one wanted to deal with that threat so soon after their last encounter.

Chapter Two

Sean planted his boot squarely on the zombie's chest and glanced at his brother. "My turn," he said as he pulled a piece of rebar with a sharpened end from his backpack.

Scott peered around his brother's shoulder. "Oh, going low-tech, eh?"

"Yep. Never can tell when you have an up close and personal with one of these guys and there's no gun or knife handy. Later I'll show you something I've been working on that's a little better than this thing."

"Don't get anything in your mouth or eyes," Scott cautioned as he stepped back.

Sean didn't reply, but he slid his glasses down over his eyes and pursed his lips tightly together. He glanced down at the zombie under his boot. From what he could tell, it was male and fairly young. Currently it was clawing at his leg and trying to bite his foot with an obviously broken jaw. There was something wrong with its legs, which had made it easy for Sean to send it to the ground with only one solid kick to the chest.

He was surprised that the overall rate of decay was so slow and the one under his foot was definitely stinking and nasty, with several gaping wounds all over his body, but for the most part was still completely intact. Positioning the stake directly over the zombie's right eye, he quickly brought down the stake, driving it deep into the brain. The zombie immediately stopped trying to fight him, becoming limp and motionless.

"No life or whatever you want to call it left in this one," Sean said nonchalantly. He took his foot off the body and gave it a nudge. "Works as well as a bullet, but a lot quieter."

Scott glanced around the street. They were back in Harris on the far side of town where no one dared go until now. He couldn't see them, but he could hear zombie moans and they were getting louder.

They obviously heard the team drive in and were headed their way. Everyone now knew that they "talked" to each other in their heads, so he knew that more and more would show up until they overwhelmed Sean and Scott's group.

He gave a low whistle. He waited until he saw everyone turn his way before motioning for them to come back. They formed a loose circle around him.

"The zombies are coming; we are going to have to move a couple blocks down and about a block over and do it fast before they see us. You all know we have to stay one step ahead or leave."

At their nods he continued, "Good, let's be as quiet as possible." He nodded toward Sean. "Will you take the lead? I'll take the rear."

Sean slung his backpack over one shoulder. He glanced at the group. "Ready?" At their nods, he turned and set off for a nearby side street.

He glanced back once and was pleased to see everyone lightly trotting silently behind him. They worked hard to train everyone on how to conduct a mission without letting every zombie around know they were there. So far they'd been very successful, pulling over thirty-five survivors from Harris and not one person was lost to a zombie attack. They had one close call when they were ambushed on a dead end street, but again their training saved them and they were able to fight their way out.

16

Most of the residents of Shady Oaks, if they were in good physical shape, belonged to one of three specific teams that went out to find survivors.

Like Shady Oaks, Harris was divided up into grids and thoroughly searched. The first team, which Sean and Scott belonged to, went in and destroyed any zombies or vicious packs of wild dogs they came across. They did not enter any buildings; their job was to move fast so they weren't swarmed. The next team established perimeters and quietly looked for survivors, including any friendly dogs and cats, and taking out any remaining zombies. The third team was on call to assist the other two teams if additional manpower was needed.

They had searched half of Harris so far and with the influx of new people from there and from Ambrose, Shady Oaks was beginning to feel like a real town again. No one was fooled though; almost every adult kept some type of weapon within arms' reach. If the church bells sounded, everyone knew where to go and what to do. Women, children, the ill, and the elderly went to the well-stocked shelter or to the secure room in the post office basement. Others

17

took up preset stations throughout town. The stations had weapons caches and other supplies, including food and water. Everyone had a BOB, or bug-out bag, packed and ready to go. Until they were able to clear all the surrounding small towns and the Connor Group was no longer a threat, no one could really relax.

Once Sean reached the street he wanted, he raised a hand and everyone took up positions around him. He pulled out a small map as Scott walked up.

"We're right here," Sean jabbed at the map with a gloved finger. "We can search this side of town and do the other side tomorrow when the nasties are gone. What do you think?"

Scott looked around and nodded. "Sounds good to me. When we come in tomorrow we might consider having the trucks drop us off in a cleared area so we don't attract our friends."

"Good idea," Sean said. He rolled up the map and stuck it back inside a pocket of his light brown jacket. He and Scott preferred to wear their Army gear, but no one else had uniforms so they settled on everyone wearing mostly earth tones to blend in better with their surroundings.

18

family. He and Charlie often butted heads and once Charlie punched him in the mouth for almost getting them all killed while fighting zombies.

"Take a seat, Charlie," Mark said amicably. He gestured toward Dexter. "Been talking to Dex here, he would like to become a deputy and I'd like your opinion."

Charlie raised his eyebrows and glanced at Dexter, who gave him a cheesy smile. Charlie wanted to roll his eyes, but managed to refrain, glancing instead at Mark. He hated being caught in the middle. "Can you clarify what you need exactly?"

Mark frowned slightly as he thought for second, and then grinned. "Let me make this easy for you. I need someone who is dependable, will be on time, and can learn quickly."

"Well, I think Dexter is dependable, he's a stickler for being on time anywhere he goes, and he is a quick learner," Charlie said slowly.

Mark smiled and leaned back in his big red leather chair. Once again his grin lit up his dark features. "That's excellent. Now tell me, does Dexter play well with others?"

31

Charlie actually felt himself squirming. Buck up, he thought to himself. He straightened and glanced again at Dexter, who was staring a hole in him.

"At times I'd say no, he doesn't play well with others." When he saw Dexter start to object, he held up a hand. "Sometimes, what's needed is a firm hand and Dexter knows how to get people moving to his commands. I know this can rub folks the wrong way, myself included, but he gets the job done and that's what we need many times."

Mark narrowed his eyes before slowly nodding. "Very good. I think you've answered my questions."

He stood and walked around the desk to stand in front of Dexter. Dexter jumped up and the two men shook hands. Mark turned to Charlie. "So we have our first new deputy, I'm going to swear him in right now. Go grab Candice, she can be another witness."

As Charlie hurried off to find Candice, he hoped Dexter would be a good addition and that their decision to make him a deputy was not a huge mistake they would regret later.

****

Sean took his time with the binoculars and slowly scanned the seemingly deserted town.

"Don't see a thing," he said in a low voice. He turned to look at his brother. "What are the others reporting?"

"Same thing. As far as they can see into the town, there's nothing."

Sean frowned and lowered the glasses. "I guess this means we need to get out and do some recon, try to figure out if they're still here and if not, where they went."

The brothers didn't have to wait for long, within ten minutes they were on the ground with a small contingent sent to scout the outskirts of Harris.

"Here's hoping we find something," Sean whispered to Scott before they spread out to comb the western edge of town. Scott nodded and waved to his brother as he moved off.

They slowly moved through the rough fields and small streams they encountered. Sean was about to give up hope of finding anything when a soldier about twenty paces ahead signaled he found something. The team rushed over.

33

The soldier was squatting down. "Look," he whispered while pointing. "Tire tracks."

Everyone immediately began searching for more tracks, which they found.

Sean trotted over to his brother. "Seems like when they left, they went north," he said in a rush. "I'm guessing there were at least five or six vehicles here."

Scott nodded. "That's what I'm thinking too."

"Well, guess we should head back and let them know what we found," Sean remarked.

Once Captain Sears was briefed, orders were quickly given. Half the platoon would continue on foot toward the mountain and the other half would bring up the rear in the vehicles. There was only one small dirt road in the area going up into the Fletcher Mountains and it was barely passable, so most vehicles would be left behind at that point. What they would find on the mountain was anyone's guess.

Sean and Scott traveled in the captain's jeep; Sean suspected that he had promised their father he would watch out for them. Sean sighed and settled back to relax for a moment since there was really nothing else he could do.

He closed his eyes and felt a poke in his side. He glanced at Scott, who was looking in the other direction. As he closed his eyes again, he felt another poke. He opened one eye. Scott was still looking out the window. "One more and I'm going to throw you out of here," he hissed.

Scott turned toward him, eyes all wide and innocent. "Pardon me?"

"You heard me," Sean growled, still looking at Scott with one eye shut.

Scott flashed him a huge grin. "Ooh, someone is crabby."

Out of the corner of his open eye, Sean noticed Sears turn toward them. He glanced back at Scott then back at the Captain. Scott followed his gaze and sat up straighter. They sat quietly until he turned back to his maps.

"Oops," Scott whispered with a soft laugh.

"You're an idiot," Sean whispered back and couldn't help but smile.

Scott winked and turned back toward the window. Sean closed both eyes and silently prayed that no matter what they found or got

into, they would all come back
safe and sound.

Chapter Four

"I'm thinking of heading over to the sheriff's office, want to come?" Mick asked Cindy as they pulled carrots from one of their garden plots in the back yard.

He straightened and arched his back to work out a kink. The yard was filled with raised beds of lettuce, potatoes, beans, onions, and carrots. He enjoyed looking at them and the young apple and pear trees they planted. He liked the yard's privacy fence even more, he felt like it offered them more security while they worked.

"Are you going over there to check on the boys?"

"That and to see if there's anything new."

Cindy looked up. "I think I'll stay here. If there's any news, tell me right away though, okay?"

Mick kissed her then smiled into her eyes. "Will do. I won't be gone long."

After checking that both their walkies were on and set to the same channel, Mick headed out. As he walked, he glanced around and smiled. Everyone worked hard to bring Shady Oaks back, and the casual observer would probably never guess what had transpired in the small town.

Homes were filling up and yards were mowed regularly. Places like the hardware store were open, but business was conducted a little differently now. They used a barter system for most items being sold, but borrowing an item was allowed, as long as it was returned in good condition. The grocery store was now used for stockpiling their non-perishable food, recently canned jars of fruits and vegetables were being added daily.

Every Saturday a small farmer's market sprung up in front of the grocery. Fresh milk, eggs, and produce were the most popular items, with beef and chicken a little harder to come by, the farms offered meat only twice a month so far. In exchange, everyone in town had to pitch in at the farms; even the older children had chores.

He was hopeful that they would continue to expand out from Shady Oaks and prosper. Perhaps one day they could attempt to clean up Ambrose, but he feared that would be years away.

Mick was so deep in thought he almost collided with Charlie at the door.

"Whoa there, partner!"
Charlie said with a laugh as he
put a hand on Mick's chest.

"Sorry about that," Mick said
with a shake of his head.
"Curiosity was getting the better
of me so I decided to come by and
see if anyone's heard anything."

"Nothing yet," Charlie said.
"Guess what?"

Mick eyed his friend. "What?"

"We have a new deputy."

"And you want me to guess who
it is, right?"

Charlie chuckled. "Yep."

Mick decided to play along.
"Okay, is it Judith?"

Charlie shook his head.

"Reggie or Travis?"

Reggie was the sheriff's son
and both men knew the teen had no
interest in law enforcement.

"Funny, you know they're too
young, and Reggie isn't even in
town right now.."

Mick rubbed the scar on his
right cheek, a permanent reminder
of his stay at Dave's Place. "Oh
yeah, I forgot he's in Ambrose. I
give up, who is it?"

"Hey, I'm not gonna let you
off that easily," Charlie quipped.
"I'll give you a hint - it's
someone I butt heads with quite a
bit."

Mick's eyes widened. "No way!"

"Yes way," Charlie said. "My old buddy Dexter was just sworn in as Shady Oaks' new deputy sheriff."

Mick groaned and Charlie chuckled at his reaction. He grasped Mick on the shoulder and gave him a light shake.

"Well, there's no news right now, want to walk some more? I'm going up to the grade school to help them finish the repairs and then check the inventory.

All three schools were small so making repairs wasn't difficult, just time consuming. When school started in the fall, Charlie wanted to be sure each child would have the books and supplies they needed.

"Sure," he said while reaching for his walkie. "Let me tell Cindy where I'm going."

Charlie started to reply when he heard a familiar voice coming from his own walkie. He quickly removed it and pressed the send button. "Hello? This is Charlie. Jenny, is that you?"

"Dad! Yes! This is Jenny!"

Charlie frowned, she sounded frantic. "I hear you; honey – what's going on – is everything okay?"

After a few seconds of static, her voice came through and this time she was whispering.

"We're in trouble," he heard her say breathlessly. "There's some kind of camp up here, a big one. Jake thinks it must be the Connor Group and they spotted us when we came up the hill. We're hunkered down behind some trees, but it's only a matter of time before we..."

Charlie heard a faint shout and groaned when only static filled the air again. He waved the walkie in the air and turned desperate eyes toward his friend. "What do we do?"

Mick was deeply worried. "Let's tell Mark and see if he can get hold of Captain Sears, maybe they could head that way."

Before he finished the sentence, Charlie was already headed back inside. Mick followed at a slower pace, wondering how he was going to tell Cindy that Brooke and the others were most likely in the hands of the Connor Group.

Absentmindedly, he rubbed the scar on his cheek and squared his shoulders. He knew they were capable of doing anything to get their daughters, Jake, and Jimmy back safe and sound. Anything.

41

****

Sean pointed over the small ridge they were sitting behind. "I can finally see the guys that walked up," he whispered to his brother. "I'm glad we got to ride most of the way, they look tired."

"They look out of shape," Scott remarked dryly as he got on his knees to take a look for himself.

Sean chuckled and Scott grinned. "True, but they probably haven't been able to do much training. All they've been doing is chasing after the Connor Group," Sean replied. He sat down again with his back against the mossy wall of the ridge and Scott joined him.

"We should be hearing something soon from the scouts," Scott said. He pulled two energy bars from one of his BDU shirt pockets and handed one to Sean.

They silently chewed and watched the other soldiers sprawled out around them. Sean noticed a young soldier strolling their way. He realized it was the same one with Captain Sears at Dave's Place, but couldn't remember his name. Quickly swallowing, he nudged Scott in the ribs.

"Heads up," he said softly.

Scott looked up and nodded. "I see him. Sears' little messenger."

"Yep."

They both remained seated and looked up when the soldier stopped before them. Sean looked at his name tag and thought to himself; yeah he looks like a Private Dooley. "Any news?" he asked.

Dooley nodded vigorously. "Scouts spotted a large camp a mile up. The Captain is certain it's the Connor Group. He said to tell you to come with me; we're leaving in five after the group that hiked up here has a chance to catch their breath."

As they rose to their feet, Scott muttered, "They need more than five to catch their breath."

Sean laughed and gave Scott a shove. "Play nice," he said with a chuckle. "These guys have been good to us."

"True, they have," Scott agreed. He slung his weapon over a shoulder and eyed Dooley. "Lead the way."

As they approached, Scott saw several men focused on a map spread out on a small folding table. Captain Sears looked up as they approached and waved them over.

Once at his side, he pointed to the map. "I'm hoping you two can shed some light on this since you're more familiar with this area. The scouts came across this large meadow and lake here," he said, jabbing a finger at the map again. "They're telling me that on the north side there's a huge camp with military style tents and even a few small wood structures. The scouts couldn't get too close because of sentries posted all around, and even with binoculars they couldn't identify who they are, but my guess is that it's the Connor Group"

Sean frowned, still staring at the map. "So you've decided to go in?"

He nodded. "We need to find out what's going on up there. Do you two have any knowledge of this area so we can surround them without being seen?"

Sean shook his head while Scott scratched his. "Sorry, we've been so busy cleaning out Harris we haven't had time to do any exploring," Sean said. "I do know it's a popular place for folks in both Shady Oaks and Harris to fish and picnic at, even though it's not that easy to get to."

44

"Sure, Mom," Sean said softly.

"Please, bring them all home safe and sound. That's all I ask," she said with tears in her eyes. She handed the walkie back to Mick and wiped her eyes.

"Sean, this is Dad again."

"Okay. Dad, I have to go, we're heading out."

Mick swallowed the lump in his throat. He couldn't believe all his children were probably in very grave danger. "Be careful, Mom and I love you. Tell Scott we love him, too."

"Will do, we love you too! I promise to contact you the minute we know anything."

Mick slowly lowered the walkie and caught Charlie's eye. Unspoken words passed between them as they both had the same thought. Mick gave a slight nod of his head toward the exit and Charlie nodded back.

Mick glanced at Cindy, who was now talking in hushed tones to Rose and Judith. He tapped her lightly on the shoulder. "I'm going outside to get a breath of air and talk to Charlie, meet me out there when you're done?"

She gave him a curious look before nodding. Mick gave her a quick kiss and headed for the

47

door. Charlie was waiting for him under the large oak tree next to the flag pole.

Charlie spoke first. "We're going, just the two of us."

"Agreed."

"We need to get things together and quickly. I'm hoping we can get up there unseen, check out the situation, and find a way to get our kids out of there."

"Captain Sears and his men create the perfect diversion, but if we tell them we're up there, he'll send us packing."

"Okay, so we don't tell them until they can't do anything about it," Charlie rubbed his chin thoughtfully. "Think I'll see if any more flash bangs are left. We need a list," he muttered. "Be right back."

Mick watched Charlie hurry over to his office. Within two minutes he was back with a small pad of paper and a pencil.

"After we figure out what we need, we can divide the list up so we can get everything faster," he said with the pencil clenched between his teeth as he flipped open the pad.

Charlie wrote quickly as they brainstormed what they needed. When he finished writing, he tore the list in half and gave the bottom portion to Mick.

"I'll get right on this," Mick said, waving the small piece of paper in the air. "Should we try to meet back here in about an hour?"

Charlie nodded, stuffing his half of the list into his shirt pocket. "What do we tell everyone?"

Mick frowned, he hadn't thought about a cover story. "Let's tell them that we're going to check the perimeter of town, just to be sure there's nothing unusual going on, and not to expect us back until late."

"But we have patrols that walk the perimeter."

"True, but we want to make sure for ourselves that everything's fine," Charlie said with a grin.

Mick grinned back and waved a finger at his friend. "That will work."

"Yep."

Chapter Five

Sean and Scott watched the activity at the mysterious camp through binoculars. They were about three hundred yards into the tree line on the backside of the camp, hidden in deep foliage right off a small animal trail. They spent the last two hours slowly and carefully circling behind and it was up to them to call in anything important. Once everyone was in place, Captain Sears planned to make his presence known and then negotiations would hopefully begin.

There seemed to be no activity on their side so Sean busied himself studying the buildings and tents. There were two large white tents with camouflage netting on top; Sean guessed it was to keep anyone who might come down from the mountain from spotting them right off. Both had generators and central air units humming away. From experience, Sean knew the tents could house just about anything in a climate controlled setting. Smaller tents flanked them on both sides.

Next he turned his attention to the buildings on his far left. One was a regular square building, probably where central command was housed. He could see only one window on the right with a small air conditioning unit jutting out. Sean knew those units tended to be noisy so any sound from outside, like Scott and himself sneaking up, would not be heard.

The next building was huge and had him puzzled. Long and rectangular, he had no idea what could possibly be in there, perhaps it was for supplies. He couldn't see any windows or a door so he assumed there was only one at the front. He nudged his brother and pointed.

"What do you think that's for?"

Scott turned his way and glanced over at the building before shrugging. "No idea, it is a weird shape, though."

Before he could reply, Sean was certain he heard a banging noise emanating from the strange building. "Scott," he hissed, nudging him again. "Did you hear that? What do you think is banging like that in there?"

Scott turned again, lifting his binoculars to his eyes. "I heard it, but still don't see anything. Do you think they're keeping Brooke and the others in there?"

Sean shook his head, eyes still fastened on the building. "Nah, they're most likely being held in one of the big tents. Do you think it could be animals? If it's the Connor Group, we know they're probably experimenting with different vaccines so they could have animals up here."

Scott lowered the glasses to look at his brother. "Could be. We should probably let Captain Sears in on this."

While Scott was on the walkie explaining what they found, Sean continued to scan the area. When he heard the banging again, louder this time, he began to grow uneasy. He had a growing suspicion that animals weren't responsible for the noises.

As he continued to watch, he saw movement at the front of the building. He swung the binoculars up in time to see two men carrying what looked like cattle prods, followed by another man in full protective gear and carrying a large black suitcase quickly enter the building. He heard the door clang shut behind them, which meant it was metal and probably reinforced.

Scott was still on the walkie and Sean scooted over to him. Tapping him on the shoulder he whispered, "Tell him I believe they're keeping zombies in that building."

Scott eyes widened in surprise, but he did as Sean asked and relayed the information. "He wants to know why you think that," Scott whispered back.

Sean filled him in on what he observed and Scott passed the information on. Scott nodded a few times then lowered the walkie.

"He wants us to keep eyes on it for now, he told me everyone's almost in position. He's very curious as to how they would get a whole building full of zombies up here."

"They had to use the main road up here, it's an old wood hauling road and rough, but a small semi could probably make it up here." Sean shrugged. "Don't really know, maybe they even herded them up here. They do have cattle prods."

Scott chuckled softly and shook his head. "Wish you could see the picture that idea put into my head. Zombie herders. Do you think they even rode horses and rounded 'em up?"

Sean made a face at his brother and they both grinned. Sean's grin quickly faded when they heard muffled shouting, then a familiar-sounding long and drawn out wail. "Oh yeah, there's definitely zombies in there."

"Wonder how many?"

Sean shrugged. "No idea, but judging by the size of the building could be a hundred or more."

Scott whistled softly then settled in next to his brother to continue their uneasy watch.

An hour slowly passed and Sean began to feel antsy. Everyone should be in position, but they'd heard nothing. He and Scott were still watching the backside of the camp and everything was quiet. Earlier, they'd heard banging and other noises coming from the long rectangular building in front of them, and they were fairly sure it contained zombies, but even that had settled down.

"What do you think is taking so long?" he asked his brother.

"Could be anything," Scott replied. He was sitting with his back against a large tree and had his eyes closed. "Take a chill pill; you know how these things go."

Sean sighed and got up on his knees so he could stretch his back. "You know how I am, I hate waiting."

A rustling sound off to their right brought them to full alert. Sean quickly scooted over behind a tree and Scott got to his knees to do the same. Both relaxed when they spotted four soldiers threading their way toward them. Sean slowly stood and gave them a quick wave. Once they reached the brothers, they quickly filled them in on what was going on.

Complete radio silence was in effect while final tweaking and placement of soldiers took place. The four soldiers would help Sean and Scott secure the back in case anyone tried to leave that way once they revealed themselves to the camp.

Once the soldiers were in place, Sean and Scott settled in again, but this time they were sitting together so they could talk.

"What do you think is happening up front?" Sean whispered.

"I'm hoping we're ready and the Captain is on his way to confront them."

"Do you think they'll give us Brooke and the others back without a fight?"

Before Scott could reply, the sound of a single gunshot rang out.

"I think that's your answer," Scott growled as he grabbed his rifle.

"Damn! I was hoping this was going to be resolved easily," Sean muttered. He walked on his knees over to another tree and looked out over the camp with his binoculars.

"See anything?" Scott asked as he joined him.

"No. Wait. I do see something." Sean adjusted the glasses. With the binoculars he could make out several figures standing between the tents. To his dismay, one man had a firm grip on Brooke's arm, another man had Jenny by an arm, and both had their hands bound together behind their backs with plastic handcuffs. Two other men stood guard on either side, one balanced a rifle on his hip and Sean figured he must have been the one that fired the shot.

He raised the binoculars slightly and refocused. Now he could make out the Captain, who was standing several feet away with his hands out.

He felt a nudge and Scott asked in a loud whisper, "What do you see?"

"Four men, two have the girls, and there are two guards.

Captain Sears is apparently still trying to talk to them," he whispered back.

"I'm moving to another tree so I can see what's going on," Scott said before moving off on all fours.

Sean focused back on the man holding Brooke's arm. He seemed to be doing most of the talking so Sean assumed he was the one in charge. Sean could only see him from the back and occasionally caught a glimpse of his profile. He was very tall and every part of him seemed long and thin. When he turned, Sean could see that even his nose was long, but shaped more like a beak than a nose. He had wavy dark brown hair tied back in a long ponytail that went halfway down his back. His clothes and watch were expensive looking, and he was wearing dress shoes.

Sean took another quick look at the man holding Jenny; he was nicely dressed and clean shaven, but a lot shorter than the man next to him. Most likely the bodyguard or second, Sean thought to himself. The other two men flanking them were obviously former military and he gave them an even faster once over. Nothing new there.

He zoomed out so he could view the entire scene. The situation didn't seem to be getting any better. Captain Sears looked perplexed and was shaking his head. Abruptly, he swung around on his heel and headed for the jeep behind him. The four men turned and led the girls back into the white tent on their right.

"Damn," Sean muttered to himself. Obviously there was a stalemate and that was bad for everyone involved.

****

Charlie was waiting at his truck outside City Hall when Mick showed up carrying a large backpack slung over his shoulders and a rifle hanging from one hand.

"Sorry it took so long," Mick apologized as he carefully placed the rifle on the grass and wriggled out of the backpack, swinging it into the back of Charlie's pickup with a loud grunt. "I'm not sure Cindy bought all this, but she didn't come right out and say anything."

"Same here," Charlie said. "Judith was giving me the look that says you're up to something. When I told her we'd be back before dark she relaxed, but not completely."

"They know us too well," Mick remarked as he opened the passenger side door and climbed in. After Charlie hopped in he said, "Cindy and I are always honest with each other, but she and Judith have enough to worry about. They're trying to locate Megan and Darrell to let them know what's happened to Jimmy and the others. If we tell them what we're going to do, they'll insist we either stay or take more people."

Charlie nodded and started the engine. They were going to take the road as far as possible before hiking the rest of the way in. Most of the town's inhabitants rode bikes or walked, but those in office still needed vehicles to be able to get around quickly if needed, so Charlie still had the pickup he inherited when he first came to Shady Oaks.

"Did you manage to get everything on your list?" he asked Mick.

"Almost," Mick said. He pulled his piece of paper out and scrutinized it carefully. "Wasn't able to get three flash bangs, but I did get two."

"Two's good," Charlie remarked as he passed the soccer

field on the way out of town. He waved at a couple of kids kicking a ball back and forth and they waved back. He sent up a quick prayer that things would continue to go well for them at Shady Oaks, but the way things were progressing he wasn't so certain.

Until they were stronger with more people residing there to help defend the town, their entire situation was tentative at best. The Connor Group could bring them all down, but at least with the military around they had a fighting chance.

Mick interrupted his train of thought. "Do you hear that?" Mick stuck his head out the window, then back in again. "That weird thrumming sound?"

Charlie slowed down and stuck his head out the window. He could clearly hear it and it was getting louder. He glanced at Mick, who had his head out the window again. "What is that?"

Suddenly Mick stiffened in his seat. "I see it! You're not gonna believe this, but it's a helicopter!"

Charlie pulled over to the side of the road, slammed on the brakes, and jammed it into park. They both jumped out of the truck.

"Over there!" Mick pointed toward the soccer field.

"I see it," Charlie said as he watched the helicopter swoop in and hover over the soccer field. He didn't know too much about helicopters, but knew it was a dual-bladed Huey Cobra, and a fairly beat up one at that.

The two kids playing there had already fled the field and were talking excitedly to one another in the parking lot.

As the chopper began a descent, clearly intending to land on the field, Charlie reached into the truck and turned off the ignition.

"Looks like our little trip will have to wait for just a bit, let's go see who that is and what they want," he yelled over the roar.

Mick nodded and together they slowly trotted toward the now stationary helicopter. They were almost there when the pilot shut down and after a moment, stepped out and waved.

"Do you know him?" Charlie asked.

"Never saw him before," Mick replied.

When they reached the stranger, he thrust out a hand and both men shook it. He was well

built with a rugged look to him
and of medium height, with short
curly black hair and brilliant
blue eyes. The women in his family
would always tell him that he
looked like the kind of guy who
should be on the cover of some
outdoor magazine. Beside that, he
immediately reminded Charlie of
someone.

"I'm Harry Jones," he said
with a smile. I've come to Shady
Oaks to see if I could find my
niece."

"Ah," Charlie said with a
grin. "I know who you remind me of
now; you're here for Bitsy, aren't
you?"

Harry nodded. "I sure am, is
she all right? Her parents made it
to our place, but we ran into
problems and unfortunately I'm all
she has left in the world now."

Charlie returned the nod
solemnly. "Sorry to hear of your
loss, but yes - Bitsy's fine.
She's quite the firecracker and
had to manage on her own until we
found her or as she tells it, she
found us."

"She's been staying with my
wife and I," Mick interjected.
"We've really enjoyed having her
around. Right now she and her
friend Travis are at one of the

62

farms fetching eggs; she'll be thrilled to see you."

Charlie glanced down the hill; several people were headed their way. "Looks like the welcoming committee is almost here." He glanced back at Harry. "Please feel free to stay here for as long as you need, I'm sure you and Bitsy need some time together. We'll make sure someone keeps an eye on the chopper for you."

With a quick glance at Charlie, Mick said, "We were on our way to check on some things, we'll make sure someone gets you over to my place where you can wait for Bitsy."

"Thank you," Harry replied. "I need to secure the chopper first, so if you'll excuse me."

Both men watched Harry for a moment until he was out of earshot.

"I see Judith leading the pack, so I'm going to ask her to escort him over to your place," Charlie said in a low voice. "Then let's get out of here."

"Okay, I don't see Cindy, she must have stayed behind. I'll get back in the truck and maybe after you talk to Judith we can make our break."

"Sounds good to me," Charlie said. Mick headed for the truck as

63

Charlie went to greet Judith and the others. He was excited about Harry Jones appearing literally out of nowhere with a helicopter, which could turn out to be something they could really use, but he was beginning to feel frustrated by all the delays.

Charlie introduced everyone to Harry then quickly said goodbye again to Judith before trotting over to the truck and hopping in.

"Phew," he said as he reached over and started the truck. He looked in the rear view mirror. "They're swarming the poor guy," he said with a chuckle as he slowly pulled away from the curb.

Mick turned to watch for a moment before turning back to Charlie and grinning. "Harry is probably wondering what he got himself into."

"He'll find out soon enough."

"What do you think his plans are? If he stays at Shady Oaks, that helicopter could sure come in handy."

Charlie reached the road leading up to the meadow and turned. "Guess we'll find out soon enough," he replied. He pointed to a spot ahead. "Sorry, to change the subject, but see that big tree? Let's stop there and go over what we have and what we're going

to do once we get up there so
we'll be ready."

Mick nodded. "Sure thing, we
definitely do need some kind of
plan."

Chapter Six

"I can't believe so many people take this hike," Charlie huffed. He glanced up at the tree-lined, meandering deer trail they walked on. He waved a hand in the air. "Okay, time for a break."

Mick spotted a fallen log and headed directly for it. He sat on one end, sighed loudly, and wiped the sweat from his brow with the bottom of his shirt. "Good timing, I was about spent," he managed to say. He quickly swung his canteen around and took a long drink.

Charlie sat down next to him and took a swig from his canteen. "Cold still, oh man that's good," he said with a chuckle. He took another drink and wiped his mouth. He watched Mick take a drink and pointed his canteen toward the path.

"See where the trail turns?" At Mick's nod he continued. "If I read the map correctly, right past that bend we should come across the meadow, so we'll have to stay within the tree line once it starts to open up."

"Do you think we'll run into the boys?" Mick asked as he screwed the cap back on his canteen. "They would be furious if they knew we were up here."

"Hopefully, if everything goes according to plan, we can be in and out before anyone knows what happened." He patted his backpack. "Our little "distraction" should see to that."

Mick grinned. "Don't know about the little part, but yeah, it should definitely work."

"Yep, I'm counting on it," Charlie said. "Well, enough jawing, let's get going."

Both men stood and after donning their backpacks, set off. To their surprise, as soon as they rounded the bend, the meadow was before them. Without a word, they both scurried for the shelter of the trees.

Once safely hidden, Charlie glanced out at the camp before them and whistled softly. "Will you look at that? We almost walked right in on them."

"The camp is huge," Mick whispered back. "How will we find them amongst all those tents?"

Charlie was stumped. He expected a small contingent, not a well established camp, and he wasn't sure how to proceed.

"There must be at least a hundred people in there, judging by all the tents," he said with a shake of his head.

Mick pointed. "See the two large white tents? Maybe they're being kept in one of those."

Charlie squinted, and then dug in his backpack for binoculars. Holding them up to his eyes, he couldn't believe what he was seeing.

"Mick, take a look at the big tents," he said in a low voice as he handed the binoculars over.

Mick adjusted the binoculars as he put them up to his eyes. "Oh my," was all he managed to say as he handed the binoculars back to Charlie and looked at him with surprise in his eyes. He couldn't believe their luck. Both girls were in front of the large white tents. Mick didn't like the fact that they were obviously being held against their will, but at least they knew where they were.

"They're talking to Captain Sears," Charlie said, watching from the binoculars again. "Oh damn, he just turned and walked away, they're taking the girls into the tent on the right."

"That's not good," Mick remarked dryly as Charlie turned and sat next to him with his back against a large oak tree. Mick picked up a twig and sighed. "If the captain can't get them back, then we'll have to go ahead with our plan." He snapped the twig and flung the two pieces into the underbrush. He turned back around to glance at the camp again while Charlie dug a jacket out of his backpack and tied it around his waist.

Mick heard a rustling coming from the underbrush where he'd just thrown the twig and assumed he scared up a rabbit or squirrel. When he glanced back, he was startled by the long barrel of a rifle pointed right at his face. Charlie sat frozen next to him. Mick swallowed and looked up at the men now surrounding them. They were all dressed in black fatigues and carried a variety of weapons.

"On your feet!" the man with the gun pointed at them growled. "Move!"

Mick swallowed hard and nodded. From the corner of his eye, he could see Charlie doing the same. They stood, hands in the air.

"Head for the camp," the man said as he gave Mick, then Charlie a shove. They both turned and headed down.

"Well, we don't have to worry about sneaking in," Charlie whispered without looking at Mick.

Mick kept his eyes straight ahead and whispered back, "That's for sure."

"Now for Plan B," Charlie said.

Mick chanced a quick glance at Charlie. He was grinning and gave Mick a wink. Mick nervously grinned back as he wondered what they'd gotten themselves into.

****

Sean swept the binoculars around the camp. He almost missed movement from the left and quickly swung back to take a better look. What he saw caused him to gasp.

"What's up?" Scott asked.

Sean lowered the binoculars and looked at his brother, a frown etched on his face. "You're not gonna believe this."

Scott frowned back. "Do tell. Like now."

Instead of replying, Sean looked through the binoculars again before shaking his head and handing them to Scott. "You gotta see to believe."

Scott growled and snatched the binoculars from his brother. After adjusting and scanning where Sean was looking, he grew suddenly still.

"Oh, tell me that's not Dad and Charlie," he groaned.

"Sorry, can't do that," Sean said with a sigh. Sean glanced around. "Where are your binoculars? I want mine back."

With another growl, Scott thrust them into Sean's hand and crawled over to his bag. After much noise and mumbling, he returned. Together they watched their Dad and Charlie being marched toward the white tents.

"This is great - just great," Sean muttered. He glanced toward his brother. "We need to get word to the Captain, but with radio silence we would have to leave our positions and we can't do that."

"Grab one of the guys chilling out around us and send them," Sean said without looking away from the scene before him. "They've reached the tents and they're going into the same one they took the girls in."

Scott snapped his fingers and rose up to look around. "Hey, remember Corporal Riley? I thought I recognized him, but just remembered his name. He's up here with us; I'll go talk to him."

As Scott went off in search of the corporal, Sean continued to watch the men escort Mick and Charlie into the tent. Once they

disappeared from view, he sighed
and scanned the area again. He
wished they knew how many men the
Connor Group had, so far he had
seen less than a dozen and there
had to be more. Perhaps they were
all inside the other big tent or
maybe they were back down in
Harris, Sean just didn't know and
it had him worried.

He shook himself from his
reverie when Scott plopped down
beside him with a grunt. "Found
him, he agreed to go."

"Good, hope we can use the
walkies soon," Sean said. His
stomach growled and Scott raised
an eyebrow. "Guess it's about
lunch time," Sean said with a
grin.

"Guess so," Scott said with a
chuckle.

Simultaneously, they both
reached for their backpacks
looking for an MRE. Scott found
his first and waved it in the air.
"Yum, looks like I'm having beef
ravioli."

Sean held his up with a grin.
"I'm having meatloaf with gravy."

Scott made a face and ripped
the meal open carefully so he
wouldn't spill the contents. "Glad
I got the ravioli, but what I'd
really like to have is the chicken
and noodles."

"Oh man, me too," Sean sighed. "The MRE ones are okay, but Mom makes the best. Let's ask her to make them when we get back, okay?"

Scott laughed. "Sounds like a plan."

Sean held up a pack of peanuts. "I didn't get candy, just these peanuts - wanna trade?"

With another laugh, Scott handed over his candy. "Sure little bro, here ya go."

Sean made a face at Scott as he popped a candy in his mouth and began to chew. "You're funny," he said after swallowing. "You know I don't eat peanuts that often."

"If that's your story..." Scott replied with a chuckle.

"It is and I'm stickin' to it," Sean chortled. He had his back to the camp facing the mountain and looked up in time to see movement on another ridge.

"Scott," Sean hissed as he dropped down to the ground. "About fifty yards up and to our left, I see movement."

Scott immediately joined him, swinging his binoculars up to scan the area. "I'm on it," he whispered back.

After a moment he lowered the glasses and gave his brother a

73

grin. "I think I see a zombie up there thrashing around."

"Oh that's just great," Sean muttered. "We better do something before it draws unwanted attention up here."

They could no longer see the heavyset and middle-aged male zombie, but could hear him crashing through the underbrush. Finally catching sight of him again, Sean slid behind a tree while Scott did the same across from him. Sean pursed his lips and let out a low whistle. Instantly, the zombie stopped and turned toward them, now making low groaning noises. To his surprise, Sean heard the zombies below him respond with groans and then they began pounding on the walls.

Scott grinned as he pulled a large branch toward him. When the zombie was close enough, he let if fly, smacking the zombie right in the middle of its chest and knocking it down.

Sean pulled out the metal rod from his backpack as he hurried over to the zombie, kicking it in the chest as it tried to get up. "Told you this would come in handy," he said softly.

"Well then, finish him," Scott whispered.

Sean gave him a quick glance and Scott nodded toward the zombie. Sean looked down at the snarling creature beneath his boot. Wasting no more time, he pressed the rod to the zombie's eye then, using his body weight, drove it deep into the skull. A thick black fluid immediately welled from the ears and mouth and fortunately for them, the zombie immediately went still.

"Flawless victory!" Scott said. He chuckled softly and patted Sean on the back.

Sean snorted. "You play too many video games," he replied. He reached down and gave the rod a hard yank to remove it from the zombie's head. Reluctantly it came free, with a loud sucking sound. As he wiped off the slimy gore from his improvised weapon in the long grass, Sean looked up at his brother, who was watching him. "We better get back to our positions."

"Yeah," Scott said agreeably.

As they walked back, Sean asked, "Did you notice the other zombies making all that noise? Seemed to me they were responding to the zombie way up here."

"I did notice," Scott replied. "Don't really know what to think of it right now. We all know they're doing some strange stuff."

As they approached their positions, they were met by Corporal Riley. "Where were you two?"

Scott jerked his head toward where they'd just come from. "Chasing a zombie, but we took care of him."

Riley's eyes narrowed for a second before he nodded. "I see. Well, we gotta get going; Capt'n wants to see both of you pronto."

Sean was relieved; he desperately wanted to know what the captain planned to do. One glance at his brother and he knew Scott was thinking the same thing. Without a word, they turned and followed Riley down the mountain.

Chapter Seven

After being manhandled into the tent, Mick first took in his surroundings and then kept his gaze on Brooke, who was sitting across from him and Charlie. She sat between Jenny and Jimmy, Jake was nowhere to be seen.

The inside of the tent was brightly lit and air conditioned, courtesy of the large generators outside. Several tables and desks with computer work stations on top were scattered throughout the area where they were now sitting on folding chairs. Behind them a plastic strip door obscured their view of what lay beyond.

Charlie leaned forward toward Jenny. "Where's Jake?" he mouthed more than whispered.

"Behind you," she whispered back. "There's a lab back there and he's trying to help them with their vaccine."

Charlie raised his eyebrows and sat back without replying. He glanced at Mick, who was still staring at Brooke and smiling. Giving him a nudge, he whispered in Mick's ear what Jenny told him.

"So they are working on a cure," Mick whispered back, never taking his eyes off Brooke. She scowled at him and he grinned. Now that he knew she was okay, he turned his full attention to Charlie. "Jake is helping, that's good, and maybe it will earn us some Brownie points."

Charlie was about to reply when an extremely tall man passed by them from behind. Abruptly he stopped and turned to face them.

He studied the group before giving them a tight smile. Then he focused on Mick and Charlie. "I imagine introductions are in order, so I will go first. I am Malcolm Greenwold, formerly from New York City."

Mick nudged Charlie, who straightened up and cleared his throat. "I'm Charlie Thompson and this is Mick Carter. We're here to get our daughters and their friends back."

"Very noble of you, coming to the rescue like that," Malcolm said with a chuckle. "Believe it or not, that is something we have in common."

Charlie tilted his head, clearly puzzled. "Really? How so?"

Malcolm walked over to a table that held Mick and Charlie's backpacks. He quickly flipped through a folder and withdrew something. Walking back over to Charlie and Mick, he showed them a photo of a handsome dark-haired boy of about fifteen. "This is my son, Connor. When the infection began, I was overseas on business. No one could tell me exactly how it happened, but Connor and several of my staff was attacked and he was bitten while being moved to a more secure location."

Charlie felt his mouth open with surprise. So Malcolm named his killing machine after his son. He slowly shook his head and glanced at Mick, who mirrored his own surprise.

Malcolm walked back to the table and replaced the photo. "Fortunately, I'm a very wealthy man. Doctors informed me that it might help to put Connor in a medically induced coma and slow his metabolism down drastically. They assured me it could be done safely so I gave the okay; it buys us valuable time in our search for a cure."

Malcolm turned. "All of you get up and follow me," he said curtly. As everyone slowly rose to their feet, Malcolm's two bodyguards stepped in with weapons in hand.

Silently the group followed until they reached the back of the tent. Charlie could make out a heavily furnished lab and saw Jake deep in conversation with a very short and squat little man with receding gray hair and thick black glasses.

Beyond them was what Charlie could only think of as a long plastic tube. To his surprise, he could make out what he assumed was the body of Connor Greenwold. He could hear a faint hissing noise, which was probably oxygen and a myriad of hoses, tubes, and wires were snaking out the bottom.

Malcolm stood next to his son's capsule and waved them all forward. He pointed to the boy's arm. "As you can see, he was bitten on the forearm. The bite is nasty looking, isn't it?" He then pointed to lines drawn above the bite. "Just like a snake bite, the doctors keep track of the infection. We have been successful in slowing it down. However, if we don't find a cure, Connor will eventually die."

Malcolm raised his head to look at them, his eyes as cold and gray as a winter sky. "I promise you though, that won't happen. I will go to the ends of the earth if I must to save my only son."

He glanced again at Charlie and Mick. "So now you see why I said we have something in common. You too would do everything in your power to save your children."

"Not if it meant killing others," Mick blurted out, but Malcolm only smiled.

"Don't be so sure about that, Mr. Carter," he said with a chill in his voice. "Those who have "helped" us with our experiments will be responsible for saving perhaps thousands of lives. Is there a nobler goal? I think not."

"You're crazy," Charlie growled, his hands opening and closing into fists. "You have caused more harm and damage than you can ever imagine. I do believe a vaccine, if not a complete cure, will be found someday, but not like this. Not experimenting on healthy men, women, and children. What you're doing will end up wiping us all out faster than the infection."

From the corner of his eye, Charlie noticed Jake and the other man watching them. He took a deep breath to try and calm himself and gave Jake a slight nod, which was solemnly returned.

Malcolm noticed the exchange and said, "Jake here has been a tremendous help and he has not been quite as judgmental. We believe he has stumbled upon a missing piece of our little puzzle that is vital to perfecting a vaccine." He motioned Jake over to

81

the group and continued. "I will let him explain to you exactly what it is we've been trying to achieve."

Malcolm stepped back and folded his arms. Jake gave him a nervous glance and Malcolm smiled. "Please Jake, do go on. Enlighten your friends of our discoveries, I am eager for them to know what we have been working on."

Charlie wasn't sure why this man was so anxious for them to understand what he was doing, but he was curious about what they knew. Perhaps this knowledge could help all of them in Shady Oaks.

Jake ran his hand through his curly red hair before replying. "All right then, I guess the best place to start is the beginning. Let's all go back up front so we can sit and be more comfortable, this will take a while."

★★★★

Sean and Scott trotted over to Captain Sears as soon as they spotted him. He gave them a quick smile.

"Now that everyone's here, we need to discuss our exchange with Mr. Greenwold and how we want to proceed," he said to the small group of soldiers assembled around him.

He wished his full company was there, but there was no way they could make it to him in time. So the smaller platoon of men he traveled with would have to do, but they were some of the finest soldiers he'd ever commanded and he couldn't ask for more.

"We've already pulled back quite a bit and I've decided to wait them out for awhile to see what they do. I didn't see many men at the camp and it's my guess that most of them are out on some kind of mission, so I don't want to wait too long. I'd like for this to be over before we have more of the Connor Group to deal with."

The captain tapped his watch while glancing at the men before him. "I am going to give them two hours before I go back. If we still have an impasse, then we will be forced to go in. Troop leaders, I will determine when the time is right to engage and most of you will probably be informed on very short notice so stay sharp and be ready."

At their nods he continued. "Everyone knows their role so I expect to see a successful mission with no civilian casualties. In case the rest of Greenwold's men do show up, we need to make sure we are not seen so that means disappear until time to act."

He gazed at the men before him. "Okay, that's all for now, you're dismissed - get your men in position and stay focused."

He turned to Sean and Scott. "You two come with me, we need to discuss what's going on with your father and the others."

Without waiting for a reply, Sears turned and headed for the jeep. Next to it was a hastily erected command center that consisted mostly of a folding table covered with maps and a ham radio, currently being operated by a grizzled, middle-aged sergeant who greeted them with a steely glare before returning to his radio. Sean grinned when Sears sat down on a case of MRE's and motioned for them to do the same.

He noticed the grin and returned it. "Gotta make do with what we have," he said with a pat to his box. "Not the most comfortable seat, but I've had worse."

"Me too, sir," Sean said with a chuckle as Scott nodded in agreement.

Sears glanced at the two young soldiers before him. "I'm

going to assume that you had no idea what your father was planning." They both shook their head and he continued. "I wish I knew what they were up to, but guess it doesn't matter anymore. Now we have six hostages to negotiate over and most likely rescue. I'm going to try one more time to secure their release, but I don't think Mr. Greenwold is willing to let them go. So what I need to know is if we have to go in, do you want to be part of the extraction team?"

"Yes sir!" They said in unison and he laughed.

"I thought you'd say that. All right then," he said, still chuckling. He pointed toward a group of men huddled around a Humvee about twenty feet away. "Go over there and tell them I sent you, they'll get you set up and briefed."

Captain Sears stood, followed by the twins. Sean reached over to shake his hand. "Thank you again for allowing us to help out, we won't let you down."

"I know you won't," Sears said as he shook first Sean's, then Scott's hand. "Your parents raised two fine young men and I'm glad to have you serve under my command at any time."

"Thank you, sir, that means a lot to us," Scott said with a smile.

Returning the smile, Sears nodded his head toward the other group. "You're welcome. Now you'd better get over there before they finish their briefing - they won't like it if they have to repeat everything."

As Sean and Scott saluted, he reciprocated and chuckled again with a shake of his head as he watched them hustle toward the other group.

Chapter Eight

Jake tapped a finger against his chin for a moment before speaking again. "As you already know, research and study of the zombies began immediately. Several interesting things quickly came to light. One of the first questions the scientists and doctors had was - why were zombies attacking people? They look like they're craving something don't they?"

At their nods, he continued. "A healthy person needs to stay hydrated, even overnight most people become slightly dehydrated during sleep. Now, let's look at a zombie. They are technically dead and they are dehydrating and drying out. What they are craving is the water that can be found in our tissue. For a short time they may be satiated, but it doesn't last long and they begin to thirst again. So they're not really hungry, they're thirsty. During their testing here, a few zombies were completely hydrated and they became totally docile. This could possibly be information we can use against them, if they're not thirsty perhaps they would no longer be a threat. They're also not interested in the moisture that could be gained from cats, dogs, or other animals - which is a good thing because some animal populations could be decimated like we were."

Mick found himself nodding. After destroying the zombies in Shady Oaks, they had to spend more time tracking down any dogs that got into skirmishes with the zombies and putting them down. Dogs could be infected, but they tended to act rabid and when the infection killed them, they did not reanimate.

"Okay, the next discovery was a little more complex and took a bit longer to figure out. One researcher's job was to watch the group of zombies being held in the building at the end of camp. He began to notice that whenever someone entered, they would all turn as one toward the door as soon as they heard the doors being unlocked. What was even more interesting, there were a few zombies being held in separate soundproof rooms. Those zombies also turned toward the door a few seconds after the main group did so. The scientists started performing several experiments and what we only guessed at they were able to confirm. Within a certain distance, they think it maxes out at two miles, the zombies definitely can communicate telepathically."

At their shocked and surprised murmurs, he held up a hand. "I know - we wondered about it, but it seems to be true. However, they don't have fully formed thoughts - it's very basic. They alert to certain sights and sounds and it gets passed around."

"I'm not so sure about that," Mick said. "We watched zombies at Dave's Place herd people toward us and then they watched our reaction when they attacked those folks. I don't want to go into what happened, but I think they're smarter than you're giving them credit for."

Charlie nodded. "I agree. The time my truck quit on us, they were definitely communicating and trying to cut us off so we couldn't get away, and we almost didn't."

Jake spun a chair around and straddled it. Leaning his arms on the back of the chair he said, "I'm just passing on what they told me, I don't think they've been studying this aspect of zombie behavior that long."

"So that takes us to the Connor Group's efforts to find a vaccine or cure. So far all efforts to develop an effective and safe vaccine have met with failure. There *is* a vaccine, but it's unreliable. From tests they've conducted, the vaccine provides protection for about sixty percent of the subjects exposed to the virus. The problem lies in the cure; the other forty percent actually die from side effects of the vaccine."

Charlie tried not to think about how many people had suffered and died so far in order for Malcolm to conduct his experiments. Malcolm was standing in the background watching them all intently. When he stood and approached them, Charlie poured as much hatred and disgust into his expression as he could muster.

"Sorry for interrupting," Malcolm said with a wave of his hand toward Jake. "There is something I'd like to elaborate. The "cure" rate is 60 percent, which is better than nothing, but what Jake hasn't been told yet is that we've been working on trying to identify those who will benefit from the vaccine. That way, over half the population could be inoculated right now. The vaccine has been tested extensively and seems to offer absolute protection. Of course we don't know how long immunity lasts, but time will tell."

Without another word, Malcolm turned on his heel and walked back to where he'd been standing earlier. Charlie shook his head and decided to ignore the irritating man.

Sure, the fact that a lot of people could be protected was wonderful news and he hoped they could find a way to tell who would benefit without killing more people, but he knew Malcolm was trying to redeem himself with his little tidbit of information.

Charlie figured Malcolm's real motive for a pretest was based more on the fact that they'd eventually run out of test subjects and not due to any sense of decency on Malcolm's part.

"That's where I come in," Jake said as he stood up. "Since we've been here and they showed me what they've been doing, I've been sharing with them what I discovered on my own. Of course, the ideal situation is to refine the vaccine so it protects over ninety percent of the population, and that's something we both are working on. But for now, it looks like we may have found the way to do effective pretesting, which means no more people will die after receiving the vaccine."

"So how did they find out so quickly you were a doctor and that you were working on the same thing?" Charlie asked.

"That's easy to answer," Jenny interjected with a grin at Jake. "As soon as he spotted all the equipment he couldn't keep his mouth shut and Malcolm scooped him right up. He's been back there ever since."

Jake stood up and nodded. "And I need to get back to work, if you all don't mind. Sorry," he said somewhat apologetically. "I want to see them succeed on this, Malcolm promised they would quit using people as test subjects if we can get this to work."

Charlie watched Jake hurry over to Jenny to give her a quick kiss before he disappeared through the plastic curtains. Malcolm pushed off a support pole he was leaning against and walked over.

"Now that you know what's going on, I'm going to send two of you out to fill this Captain Sears in on what we're trying to achieve here. The last thing I need is for them to disrupt our work. You probably thought I'd say *destroy* our work, but he won't be able to accomplish that objective. I'm sure you've noticed there are not many men here; most of them are busy carrying out their missions."

Malcolm sat down on the chair vacated by Jake and glanced at each person in turn. "If the military is still here by the time my men return, he and his entire platoon will be destroyed, so make sure he understands the gravity of the situation."

"As for those of you who remain, I will keep you safe, that much I promised Jake, so consider yourselves fortunate. I will put you to work, however; everyone here earns their keep."

Malcolm stood and glowered down at them. "Now to pick the two of you who will be leaving us?"

****

Cindy sat quietly next to Judith and tried to pay attention to what Harry Jones had to say, but she couldn't take her mind off the fact that Brooke and the others were in danger. By the look on Judith's face, Cindy realized she was also deep in thought and reached over to pat her hand reassuringly. Judith gave a small start and gave Cindy a guilty smile.

"Sorry," she whispered. "I am so worried right now."

"Me too," Cindy replied. She gave a slight nod toward the door. "Let's excuse ourselves and go outside, all right?"

"Sounds like a plan," Judith said with a nod.

Cindy glanced around her living room, which at the moment was packed with people eager to hear Harry's story of how he came to be at Shady Oaks. She stood and grabbing Judith by the forearm, pulled her up.

"Need a little air, carry on without us," she said quickly with a wave of her hand and a quick smile for Harry. They wove their way through the crowd as fast as they could and both exhaled loudly when they exited onto the broad front porch.

They stood quietly for a moment, surveying their surroundings before Judith sighed and sat down on the front steps.

"I am hoping to hear from the boys at any time," Cindy said as she joined her friend. "We haven't heard anything from Mick or Charlie, either and they promised to stay in touch." She carefully set the walkie down between them and patted it. "The boys are probably radio silent, but hopefully it won't be much longer."

Judith glanced at her friend's worried face. "I'm thinking positive; they will call in and let us know everyone and everything is just fine. As for Mick and Charlie, I'm sure they've lost track of time as usual."

Cindy nodded in response then straightened her spine when she felt something rub against her back. Smiling, she turned and picked up the small purring creature. "Moses! I was wondering where you were!"

Judith pointed at the gray tabby now sitting on Cindy's lap. "Don't you think it's strange how there were no cats around until we startled settling into the houses. Then they seemed to appear out of thin air and went about their business like nothing happened."

Cindy grinned at the still purring cat on her lap. "I agree, it was strange, it's like they hid out until things settled down then came strolling back in demanding dinner."

Judith laughed and reached over to scratch Moses behind his ears. The cat responded by purring louder, making them both chuckle.

She sighed again as she gazed out over the yard and beyond. "I

really don't think I can sit here
and wait for something to happen."

"Well, what should we do?"
Cindy gently placed the cat on the
porch and stood up to face her
friend. "Would take us a while to
find Mick and Charlie, and it
would be dark before we even got
close to the lake if we went up
there."

"Yeah, it's too bad we
couldn't fly up there and back,"
Judith grumbled. Suddenly her eyes
widened and she jumped up
excitedly. "Hey! We can't fly, but
we know someone who can!"

Cindy's mouth opened in
surprise. "Are you serious? Do you
really think he would?"

Judith was already reaching
for the door. "We won't know
unless we ask!"

Cindy scurried up the steps
and quickly followed Judith
inside. Harry was no longer the
center of attention, the group had
broken up and were now chatting in
small groups. She waited just
inside the door while Judith
threaded her way back over to
Harry, where she bent and
whispered in his ear. He gave her
a quick grin, nodded, and stood up
to follow her out.

Cindy gave him a smile when
they approached and she stepped

aside, holding the door for them to go through first.

Wasting no time, Judith turned to Harry. "We have a big favor to ask of you."

Harry raised his eyebrows as he gave her a quizzical look.

"You met Charlie and Mick earlier today, when you first landed. They were on their way to check with our people out on the perimeter of town because there's a group of mercenary-type people up on Fletcher's Mountain who are very dangerous. They took Cindy and Mick's daughter," she said with a wave toward Cindy. "They also have Charlie's daughter and both their boyfriends, and for some reason they're holding them hostage."

Cindy watched as Harry raised his eyebrows even higher. "There's a few military platoons around still, one of them we are friendly with," Cindy interjected. "My two sons went up there with them to find out what's going on and we haven't heard from them," she said with a tremor in her voice that surprised her.

She realized she was a little more distraught than she cared to admit. She gave herself a mental shake and looked directly into Harry's eyes. "We'd like to ask you to consider flying up the mountain to take a quick look, assess the situation if it's possible, and then come back and let us know what you saw. You may be able to give us an idea of what we need to do to help them up there."

Harry rubbed his whiskered chin thoughtfully as he gazed at each woman. "I would love to help you out, but I'm almost out of fuel. Also, I'd like to have a co-pilot if that's possible. I did some modifications to the Huey so it would be easier to fly on my own, but another pair of hands would help a lot."

Both women glanced at each other, frowning, before Judith snapped her fingers and grinned. "I do know where we may be able to get some fuel, but we'll have to go up to where Bitsy and Travis are, the farmer there has a small hangar on his property - if I remember right he does some crop dusting for other farms in the area."

"We'll need to grab some fuel cans from the hardware store, it's on the way," Cindy said as she headed down the steps.

"How long is it going to take to get the fuel and get back?" Harry asked as he followed her.

"This probably doesn't need saying, but I need to be up there before dark to be of any use, and if you know of someone who can go with me they can show me where to go."

Cindy stopped and turned to face him. She glanced at Judith then looking past her friend, she chuckled. Puzzled, both Judith and Harry turned to follow her gaze.

They watched the Mark emerge from Cindy's house and head straight for them. He looked up and stopped to see all three of them smiling at him. "Umm, what's up?" Mark asked, smiling slightly himself.

Cindy walked up and tapped him lightly on the chest. "You are," she quipped with a chuckle at the confused look on his face and tapped him again. "Or rather, you will be."

Judith walked over and took him by the arm. "We need you to do us a little favor..."

Watching the two women, Harry shook his head and followed along as they explained their plan to Mark.

Chapter Nine

Mick knew Malcolm would pick either him or Charlie to be one of the two to go outside, and it had to be him. If he picked Charlie, their plan would go right down the toilet, as Dexter was fond of saying. Almost before he could think it through, he stood up.

"I want to go, I believe my sons are out there and I want to make sure they're okay and that they stay out of this mess," he said in a firm voice while staring right into Malcolm's eyes.

"I see," Malcolm said calmly, raising an eyebrow as he thought about Mick's statement. "Perhaps you've come to your senses and realize the work we're doing here is important?"

Mick swallowed and slowly nodded. "Um, sure. I can see that this research could help a lot of people." He didn't dare say more; afraid he would give away his true dislike of the man and his ideas.

"I'm feeling generous, so I will agree to let you go," Malcolm said with a small smile. He looked at the group sitting around him. "Anyone else want to volunteer?" He looked pointedly at Brooke. "Except for you, I'm sure you understand why I would have to say no."

Brooke glared back for a moment before turning away with her arms folded and a frown on her face. Malcolm chuckled and once again glanced around. "Anyone?"

Mick noticed Charlie and Jenny were staring at one another. Charlie nodded slightly and she shook her head and frowned. Then she turned and looked at Jimmy, then back at her father. Charlie sighed softly and nodded again. Jenny grinned and without looking, shoved her elbow hard into Jimmy's side, causing him to shout and jump to his feet. Seeing his chance, Mick grabbed Jimmy's arm and turned to Malcolm before the boy could speak.

"All right, you have two of us. We'll tell Captain Sears exactly what you said."

"Make sure he understands that my men will be back before dusk. He needs to be gone by then," Malcolm remarked curtly. He waved a hand toward the entrance. "After you."

Giving Charlie one more meaningful glance and receiving a tiny smile in return, Mick gave a curt nod to Malcolm and still gripping Jimmy by the arm, headed outside with Malcolm on their heels.

Two men outside tensed when they saw Mick and Jimmy emerge, but at Malcolm's appearance they both relaxed but continued to stay vigilant, watching their every move.

Malcolm addressed the guards. "Escort these two to the edge of camp and let them go; they carry a message intended for the good Captain."

Malcolm spun on his heel and retreated back into the tent. One of the men nudged Mick with his rifle. To Mick, he looked like an angry bullfrog, short and squat with large bulging brown eyes. The other guard was a lot younger and taller, almost pleasant looking with a round face, freckles, and bright blue eyes under an unruly mass of blond hair.

"You heard the man, get going," Bullfrog growled, giving Mick another nudge.

Mick held up a hand. "All right, stop poking me with that thing, we're going."

Mick turned and headed for the open meadow and Jimmy followed close behind. To his surprise, the other guard ran in front of them and stopped. "No! Not that way!"

At their quizzical look, the young man swallowed and glanced at Bullfrog before continuing. "No one goes into the meadow or near the lake, Malcolm's orders." He pointed to their right. "We walk around."

Mick shrugged and gave Jimmy a quick glance before turning to the young man. "No problem, would you like to lead?"

He swallowed again and nodded. "Sure, follow me, but no funny stuff."

"You got it," Mick said with a shake of his head.

The meadow was large and it took them nearly forty minutes to travel halfway around. Mick saw several military vehicles parked along the tree line, but no one was in sight. Bullfrog raced ahead of them and held up a hand for them to stop.

"This is where we part ways," he growled, using his rifle to point toward the vehicles. "Go."

Without a word, Mick once again grabbed Jimmy by the arm and propelled him along at a rapid pace. He could feel the guards' eyes boring into their backs and he wanted nothing more than to get away from their stares and their guns. Wouldn't do to be shot in the back at this point - wouldn't do at all.

To his relief, as soon as they reached the first jeep a young soldier stepped out from behind a tree and motioned them forward. Once they reached him, it seemed as though several pairs of hands grabbed them and shoved them further into the trees.

Suddenly no one was shoving them and they both staggered and stopped. They were surrounded by soldiers, but Mick only had eyes for Sean and Scott, who were flanking the captain and solemnly staring at them.

Captain Sears strode forward and gave them a big smile. First shaking Mick's hand and then Jimmy's he said, "Our scouts saw you coming, I'm surprised Malcolm would let anyone go."

"He has a message for you," Jimmy replied.

Mick raised an eyebrow in surprise as he glanced at the boy, but decided to let him talk. Jimmy seemed to have gained back some of his courage since they were once again among friends and Mick let him run with it. To tell the truth, he was happy to let Jimmy deliver the message while he talked with his sons.

As they approached, he stepped back and waved them over. After receiving a big hug from both of them, he looked them over carefully.

"Looks like you two are okay," he said with a grin. "Your mother and I were worried about you."

Sean's smile turned into a frown. "Is that why you're up here? Do you have any idea what was going through our minds when we saw you and Charlie being marched inside that tent?"

"I can't believe Mom would let you come up here," Scott interjected. At the look on Mick's face, his eyes widened. "Does Mom know?"

Mick shook his head and to his chagrin, dropped his eyes to the ground like a child caught with their hand in the cookie jar. He looked up at their disapproving faces.

"No, we didn't tell anyone. We're supposed to be checking on the patrols around town."

Not liking the feeling he was experiencing, he raised his head and jutted out his chin. "Now you two can quit looking at me like that, you're my sons and I have every right to make sure you're

105

okay, even if it meant doing a little sneaking around."

They looked at each other in surprise and then Sean frowned again. "A little sneaking around?" he repeated. "What you did could have put this mission in jeopardy."

At Mick's stricken look, Sean softened his voice and put an arm on his father's shoulder. "Look, we know you were only trying to help, and we appreciate that."

Scott nodded and Sean continued. "But you have to realize that we're grown men now, not little kids, and we do know how to take care of ourselves. I know that sometimes it might not seem that way because we like to joke around so much, that's just our way of coping, but when we're on a mission or protecting our family or friends, we're all business."

Mick sighed. "I know. In my head, I know. But in here," he said while tapping his chest. "I don't know. When I see you two head off to do something I know is probably dangerous, it takes everything inside of me to not run after you and try to stop you."

Mick nodded toward the men assembled around Jimmy. "Let's drop this for now; I'm sure you two don't want to miss everything."

At their nods, Mick let out a small sigh of relief as they turned and he quietly followed his sons back to the group. He allowed himself to think for a moment about everyone back at the tents and crossed his fingers that the plan he concocted with Charlie would work. Heck, it had to work, Mick thought grimly, or they were all in big trouble.

****

Two farm dogs, one a rotund beagle and the other a lively and much younger border collie, escorted Cindy's truck with sharp barks and baying all the way down the drive to the McKenzie home. Driving past the house, she pointed ahead.

"This is a big farm and for now they produce most of the meat we get. There are two barns and three big fenced areas for the chickens and pigs, with the cattle in a couple of pastures up by the hangar."

She glanced at Harry, who was sitting beside her, before dodging a large dip in the dirt road. Judith and Mark were behind them in the fairly roomy back seat of the king cab having a quiet discussion of their own. "We should run into Bitsy and Judith's son, Travis, and Mr. McKenzie should be with them."

Harry nodded, leaned forward, and squinted. He pointed toward a battered white pickup parked next to the last barn. Both barns were painted the traditional red with white trim and he was impressed at how neat and in good repair everything appeared.

"Think that could be them?"

"Hope so, I don't want to spend any more time trying to find them."

Cindy pulled up next to the other truck and as she shut the engine off and looked up, saw Bitsy and Travis round the corner of the barn, each carrying a cardboard box full of cartons of eggs for the town. Following behind was Mr. McKenzie, who spotted them first as they piled out of the truck and headed their way.

The farmer waved and when Bitsy looked up and saw her uncle, she stopped dead in her tracks and would have dropped the box she was carrying if not for Mr. McKenzie's quick thinking. One look at her and he reached over and took the box from her. She let out a combination of a squeal and a scream and flew toward Harry.

Throwing herself at him, Harry scooped her up and gave her a long hug. Cindy felt tears spring to her eyes when she heard Bitsy sobbing into Harry's neck. Everyone stood quietly until Bitsy pulled back to stare into her uncle's face.

"I can't believe it's really you!" she exclaimed, her eyes wide and her face wet with tears. He set her back on her feet and she clutched his arm, still staring at him. "When and how did you get here?"

"I got here by helicopter and then these fine people brought me out here," he said with a grin toward Cindy and the others. He glanced back toward Mr. McKenzie. "They need my help, but I need fuel. We were hoping you might have some to spare."

At the farmer's nod, he grinned, walked over and held out a hand. "By the way, I'm Harry Jones and it's nice to meet you."

Further introductions were quickly made and after grabbing the gas cans from the truck bed, the group quickly hurried over to the fuel tanks. Within ten minutes all the cans were full. Placing the last can in the back, Harry turned to Cindy. "If it's all right, I'd like to ride back with Bitsy and Travis."

"Oh certainly," Cindy said with a big smile. She gave Harry a pat on the shoulder. "Besides, I don't think Bitsy will let you out of her sight for awhile and I know you have a lot of catching up to do."

"We do, I know she's going to ask me what happened to her parents and aunt, and that's one story I'm not looking forward to telling, but she has a right to know. My wife, Lana, and Bitsy's mom and dad were watching me from a nearby building while I was getting the Huey ready for flight. There were no zombies anywhere, so when I finished my preflight checks I motioned for them to come to me. I guess the noise drew the zombies out from somewhere close by and before I knew it, they were surrounded and literally torn to pieces right before my eyes."

Harry took a shaky breath and continued. "There was nothing I could do. When even more of those things headed my way I had no choice but to fly out of there. I didn't have enough fuel to get far, unfortunately. I think I was in shock; the first few days are a blur and some things I don't remember. I did manage to find enough fuel to get here, my one and only goal was getting to Bitsy, so here I am."

Cindy shook her head, closing her eyes for a second before replying. "I'm so sorry for your loss, what a horrible thing to witness. Please, have Travis drive and try to go easy on the details for her sake."

Harry nodded and sighed as he looked up toward the sky. He rubbed the back of his neck. "I've

111

been practicing what I would say all the way here and there's really no way to make it easy on her. Their deaths were gruesome and painful; the only comfort I can give her is that it was fast."

"Concentrate on that then, and spare her the other details, that should help. If she really wants more she'll ask."

"Good idea," he replied. He glanced over at Bitsy waiting with Travis at the other truck. "Guess we'd better head out then. We'll follow you out."

"Sounds good," Cindy said with a nod as she turned to get into the truck.

Within moments they were headed back to town to fuel up Harry's helicopter and get it in the air before dusk.

As she drove, Cindy told Judith and Mark what Harry told her about Bitsy's parents and his wife.

"That's awful," Judith said with a shake of her head. "So many people have lost so much, we're lucky to have some place to go that's safe."

"At least for now," Mark said in a low voice. He was sitting alone in the back and when Judith turned to look at him and Cindy gave him a quick glance through the rear view mirror, he held up his hands.

"Hey, it's the truth. We have no idea how safe we really are and we have no clue how many zombies are out there, either."

"I see what you're saying," Judith remarked. "The way I like to look at it is the farther we can drive them away or outright kill them, the better it is and right now as far as we know the closest zombies are in Harris."

"And our teams are busy cleaning up Harris, too," Cindy said with a smile.

"Well, I hope you ladies are right because I've had enough of zombies to last several lifetimes."

"Amen to that," Cindy remarked while Judith nodded in agreement.

They were silent for a moment before Judith glanced at her watch then turned toward Cindy. "How long has it been since you heard from Mick? I just realized I haven't heard from Charlie for over two hours now."

"We've been so busy I haven't even thought about it, but I haven't heard from Mick, either."

"I'm hoping they're back, how long does it take to check on a few patrols?" Judith said as she settled back against the seat.

"Knowing those two, all day," Mark interjected with a chuckle.

Chapter 10

Once everyone was briefed, they began to brainstorm on the best way to handle Malcolm and his men.

"Malcolm says his men will be back around dusk, so obviously we need to move before then if we're going to do anything to rescue his hostages," Captain Sears said as he walked back and forth. "However, he will be expecting that, and it does put the hostages in extreme danger."

He stopped and faced the men. "Ideas?"

Mick stood up from the MRE box Sean gave him to sit on. "I haven't told you yet, but Charlie has a little surprise for Malcolm, and at my signal he will put it into effect."

The captain raised an eyebrow. "Really? When were you planning on sharing this little bit of information?"

"I wasn't sure we would need Charlie, but it looks like we may have no alternative." Mick swallowed hard, so many people staring at him made him nervous, even Jimmy looked surprised.

"Charlie has a flash-bang strapped to the inside of his calf; he said they would probably miss it there and sure enough they did."

"So what is the signal Charlie will be waiting for?"

"We were watched closely so talking was nearly impossible, but we managed to formulate a quick plan. We got lucky that we weren't caught, but Malcolm likes to talk a lot. When he wasn't paying close attention, we saw our chance and took it."

He glanced around at the men, who were watching him intently. "We need to honk twice," Mick said nervously. "Was the only thing we could think of that wouldn't unduly alarm Malcolm."

Captain Sears nodded. "Okay, easy enough. Is that all?"

"After my honk, Charlie will wait thirty minutes before setting off the flash-bang. So if that will help, your men should probably be in position when it goes off. Hopefully everyone will be disoriented and we can get Brooke and the others out safely."

"We can do that," Sears said thoughtfully. "We can send some men through the meadow and the rest around the perimeter until everyone is in place, then we can give the horn on one of the supply trucks a couple taps."

Mick jumped when without warning, Captain Sears began barking orders. There was a flurry of activity as they shouldered their weapons and backpacks full of what Mick figured was ammunition and supplies. He watched a soldier head toward the meadow and when he reached the edge, dropped down and began to crawl his way through the tall and very thick grass.

When he disappeared from view, Mick began to turn away but noticed a sudden disturbance in the grass and thought he heard a muffled cry. He gazed out over the open field and listened for a moment, but saw and heard nothing else. Shrugging, he decided to make himself useful and began grabbing the MRE boxes and stacking them next to one of the small supply trucks.

Jimmy wandered off with a few of the younger soldiers, he had mumbled something to Mick about helping them with some chore. He looked up and grinned as Scott and then Sean, joined him. They worked silently for several seconds, and when Mick tossed the last box into the truck, Sean pointed toward another truck further down.

"Dad, when it's time for us to move in, you're going to be in that truck."

At Mick's frown, he grinned and continued. "Don't worry, you're not being left out - trust me, you'll be busy enough." He quickly explained that Mick was the one who would signal Charlie and then he would have the task of monitoring any communications that came across.

"All right," Mick said somewhat reluctantly. He didn't mind his assigned tasks, but knew his sons would be out in the field and wanted to be with them.

Seeing he was less than enthusiastic, Scott gave him a grin and a playful shove. "C'mon Dad, you know how dangerous this is, Mom would kill us if anything happened to you. Besides, we really need someone to listen to their chatter and let us know what's going on."

"We know how you feel, though," Sean interjected. "We always want to see action and we barely get to. I think that Captain Sears is afraid to face the wrath of Mom if anything happened to us, but it doesn't mean we like it, either."

Mick sighed and nodded. "I see your point and I know you're

right. I'll do my part as long as you two promise me to be careful."

"You got it," Scott said as Sean nodded. "The goal is to get all of us home safely."

"Yeah, so your Mom can kill me," Mick grumbled. As his sons laughed, he continued, "Seriously though, we do have what I believe is a good plan and with a little luck everything should go great."

"Think we'll need a more than a little luck, but I think we both agree with you," Sean replied as Scott nodded vigorously.

As he followed them down to the truck he would be staying in, he tried to believe what he just said, but couldn't help but worry. He knew from experience that things rarely go according to plan. As he hopped in the truck and gave his sons a thumb up before they turned and went to get ready for their mission, he realized that once again he had no real control over what was about to unfold and the thought terrified him.

★★★★

"I think we're ready to go!" Harry said with a grin as he tousled his niece's hair. Bitsy laughed and stepped back beside

Travis, who put his arm around her shoulders. Harry raised an eyebrow, which caused her to turn red. He chuckled and glanced at the Mark, who looked visibly nervous.

"Don't worry," he said as he clapped the sheriff on the shoulder and steered him toward the passenger side. "We won't go that high and I think you'll enjoy the ride."

"I hope so," Mark mumbled. He was always nervous before flying, but once up in the air he usually felt fine. "Let's get this show on the road," he said with a brave, small smile as he climbed inside.

Harry gave him another reassuring pat and shut the door. He quickly jogged back to the other side and climbed in. Once they were buckled up with their headsets on, he started the engine. A small group once again assembled nearby, eager to watch the takeoff. Bitsy and Travis moved further back and waved along with the rest. She didn't want him to leave, until he explained to her what he was doing. She didn't like it, but realized it was important and that he'd be back soon.

Harry tapped Mark on the knee to get his attention. "Before we head for this lake on the mountain, can you show me where the patrols are? Cindy and Judith asked that we check on Mack and Charlie."

Mark laughed. "Sure, we can check on *Mick* and Charlie."

"Oh, sorry about that," Harry said in a loud enough voice to be heard. He chuckled. "Glad you corrected me on that."

"No worries," Mark replied jovially. "Mick's such a nice guy he would never take offense."

"Good to know," Harry responded as he began to lift off. Both men were silent until they were in the air.

Mark pointed to the left. "We should probably start over in that direction."

"Gotcha."

Scanning the different patrol areas took less than twenty minutes. When they finished, Mark was frowning.

"I never did see the truck or any sign of either of them," Mark said as he lowered the binoculars strung around his neck. "I'm worried, especially since no one has been able to raise them on a walkie, either.

"Do you want to look again?"

Mark rubbed his chin, still looking at the ground. He suddenly looked up at Harry and snapped his fingers. "Damn! I think I might know where they are! If my hunch is right, we need to follow the dirt road up to the lake. I'll bet you anything they snuck up there!"

"Show me the way," Harry said.

"We're close to the road, keep going straight," Mark instructed.

Within a few minutes, Mark pointed. "There it is, goes about halfway up the mountain then turns into what is basically an animal trail, but we can keep following that until we get up to the lake."

Harry nodded and guided the chopper up the road. Both men were silent as they scanned the area.

"There's the truck!" Mark shouted. "Right before the road runs out, do you see it?"

"Sure do," Harry said with a nod. He once again scanned the area. "After what I've learned about this Connor group, I'm not too eager to just fly right into what could be the proverbial hornets' nest, so let's go slow on this."

"Whatever you say," Mark said agreeably. "Might be best to come up from the south then, so we need to go off to the left and then fly straight for about a mile, which

122

should put us near the lower part of the lake."

Harry made a slow turn and as they continued to scan the area for any signs of life, Mark hoped Mick and Charlie weren't in any danger; he fervently wanted to find everyone safe and sound so he could ease Cindy and Judith's worries. He sighed and leaned back against the seat. Who was he kidding? Knowing them as well as he did, he knew his friends were most likely right in the thick of it, he could only hope he and Harry could find some way to help resolve this difficult and dangerous situation without anyone getting hurt, or worse, killed.

Chapter 11

Mick impatiently tapped the steering wheel and fidgeted in his seat. He hated waiting, especially when no one was keeping him updated on what was transpiring. He glanced at the walkie lying next to him on the seat. He wished there were some way to contact Cindy, he knew they'd been gone too long without checking in and she and Judith would be worried, but with radio silence still in effect he didn't dare chance a call. He almost jumped out of his skin when Sean popped up right beside him.

"Whatcha doin'?" his son yelled in his ear before stepping back and grinning.

"Oh, you're a hoot," Mick grumbled. Unable to help himself, he grinned back. "I'm sitting here trying to stay calm and you're not helping one bit, I almost had a heart attack."

"Sorry 'bout that, here ya go," Sean said in a muffled voice as he bent down and disappeared from view. When he reappeared he had a portable ham radio with him. "You're supposed to monitor the bad guys."

Mick reached through the window to retrieve the radio and

carefully set it down on the seat next to his walkie. "At least this'll give me something to do."

Sean leaned forward. "Yep, if you hear anything at all, be sure to let us know immediately. You're supposed to contact us via the walkie on a certain frequency and only for really short messages." He thrust a small piece of crumbled paper at Mick. "Here, it's all written down."

"Thanks," Mick mumbled as he took the paper and smoothed it out on his thigh. He carefully placed it next to the radio, and then looked at his son. "Anything else I need to know?"

Sean nodded and looked down at his watch. "Wait for it..."

Mick was puzzled. "Wait for what?"

"Wait for it..."

Mick tilted his head and watched his son. Sean held up a finger for a few more seconds then pointed at Mick and yelled, "Okay, now! Honk the horn twice!"

Startled, Mick pounded on the horn without even thinking. He frowned. "You know, you could have told me it was time without all the theatrics."

"True, but it wouldn't have been as much fun," Sean quipped. "I have to get back now; Scott and

I are supposed to be with Captain Sears, everyone will be moving in quickly now to get in place before that flash-bang goes off."

"Okay, but what about Jimmy, where is he?"

"He's fine, we have some guys keeping an eye on him, we should probably just leave him with them until this is over."

"Sounds like a plan, thanks for getting him somewhere safe."

Sean nodded. "No problem, talk to you soon!"

Mick watched Sean scurry down the dirt road and around a bend where the tree line obscured his view. Sighing heavily, he leaned back and closed his eyes for a moment to try and relax. Sean had startled him more than he cared to admit and his heart was still racing. The whole situation had him unnerved and he was ready for it to be over.

He glanced down at his watch, they had synchronized watches earlier and there were only twenty minutes to go. Like his son and many others, he'd taken to wearing one of his old watches again, since they no longer used cell phones to check the time.

To his surprise, he heard a faint crackle emanate from the

radio. He really hadn't thought he would hear anything from Malcolm's men. He quickly reached over and turned up the volume. He froze, his hand still on the dial, as a voice came over loud and clear. He listened for a moment and once he realized what was being said, he felt the blood drain from his face and his heart began to race once again.

He grabbed the walkie and turned it on, quickly finding the correct frequency. He began shouting into the walkie and when he received no reply, fumbled for the door handle and almost fell trying to get out of the truck, but hurriedly righted himself. Without shutting the door or looking back and still shouting into the walkie, he ran down the road as fast as his legs would carry him.

****

Charlie was so lost in thought that for a moment he wasn't sure he heard the honks, but judging from the reactions of everyone around him, he knew they heard it. He noted the time on his watch and patiently waited another five minutes before standing up and waving in Bullfrog's direction.

Bullfrog glared at him. "What?"

"Need the bathroom."

Rolling his eyes, the big man heaved himself out of the metal chair he was sitting in next to the entrance. He waved Charlie over.

"Don't try anything," he growled. Grabbing Charlie roughly by the arm, he turned toward his younger cohort who was sitting on the other side. "Be right back, make sure you watch 'em," he said with a nod toward the group.

After receiving a nod in return, he grunted and shoved Charlie through the opening. They took a right and walked behind the tent past a large flatbed truck, then walked toward the tree line where a row of portable bathrooms stood.

Charlie headed for the closest one and without a word, quickly went inside and latched the door. He sat down and pulled up his pant leg to reveal the flash-bang strapped to the inside of his calf. He jerked the strap free and stuffed the strap and the flash-bang into the inside pocket of his jacket. Right before they were caught, he tied the jacket around his waist and quietly slipped it on after hearing Mick's signal. Standing up, he eyed the toilet and then with a shrug, quickly relieved himself, no telling when he'd have another chance.

After slathering on hand sanitizer from the dispenser, Charlie opened the door and almost got a fist in the face. "Was just gettin' ready to knock, took you long enough," the burly man growled.

"Sorry," Charlie mumbled as he brushed past the man. He kept his head down and hurried along the well-worn path back toward the tent. Once inside, he noted that Malcolm was gone and decided to sit in the chair vacated by Mick. Now he was closer to Jenny, he wanted to let her know what was going to happen if he had the chance.

Fifteen minutes to go, he thought to himself after glancing at his watch again. He leaned forward a bit, trying to catch Jenny's eye. When she finally looked his way, he put a finger to his lips as he opened up his jacket to reveal the flash-bang in his inner pocket. Jenny's eyes widened with surprise as her mouth dropped open. He frowned and shook his head slightly. She quickly sat up and shut her mouth, still looking surprised.

Charlie looked around and certain no one was watching, he softly whispered, "Fifteen minutes, pass it on."

With a slight nod, Jenny eased back in her chair and leaned sideways toward Brooke and whispered in her ear. Charlie watched as her expression matched Jenny's when he'd shown her the flash-bang. Brooke nodded. Since Jake was in the back, there was no way to warn him, Charlie planned to run back and grab him as soon as the flash-bang went off. He was betting the doctors and scientists wouldn't stop him, then they could run back up and get everyone out with what he hoped was Mick and Captain Sears' help.

His eyes darted around the room - where should he throw the thing? They were sitting almost in the center of the tent and he wanted it nowhere near them. He eyed Malcolm's men sitting at opposite sides of the entrance. He decided to pitch it in between them; it should incapacitate them long enough.

Glancing once again at his watch, he sighed. Five minutes to go. He mouth suddenly went dry and he swallowed hard. He never actually used a flash-bang before and frankly was scared of how it would turn out. He didn't want to be responsible for someone being injured or worse. Dexter showed him how to use it when they first came to Shady Oaks to find Jenny, but to actually throw one was a different story altogether.

He remembered how loud the one Dexter used in the basement of the apartment they searched was, and he had been two floors up. That thought brought back bad memories and he frowned. They just discovered a zombie when the flash-bang went off and it attacked Charlie and scratched Gordon, who became infected. When Gordon turned, he killed his wife and took off, which prompted a search for him because he still held a key to some medical supplies they needed. Charlie hoped there were no surprises when this flash-bang went off.

Shaking himself from his reverie, he looked up to see Jenny giving him a quizzical look. He gave her what he hoped was a reassuring smile and she smiled back. He pointed to his watch without looking away and after Jenny glanced down at hers, she gave him a nod and held up two fingers. He nodded back and slowly hunched forward so he could reach into his pocket without being seen very clearly.

With one minute left, he slowly reached in his pocket and carefully brought the device out and held it down between his legs. Turning his wrist, he watched the seconds wind down. With a deep breath and before he could think about what he was doing any further, he gave his daughter a quick glance before pulling the pin and heaving the flash-bang over her head.

Chapter 12

Mick almost fell twice before finally spotting a group of men huddled together on the ground pouring over a map. He skidded to a stop and as they turned surprised faces up to him, gasped out, "Captain Sears, where is he?"

"Thanks," he said with a wave of his hand as one solder pointed down the road and told him to keep going around another bend in the road, where he should find the captain. Without another look, he sprinted away, breathing heavily. Adrenaline and pure fear drove him on; he felt he couldn't get there soon enough.

To his relief, as soon as he rounded the corner he saw Sean first and then Scott. That meant the captain was close by and he frantically scanned the area. He spotted him as Sean walked over.

"Dad, what are you doing here?"

To his surprise, Mick brushed Sean aside in his hurry to talk to Sears. "No time! Have to talk to the captain right now!"

One look at his father's frightened face and Sean knew something was up and followed him. Scott noticed the odd exchange and joined them as Mick raced up and

133

jerked the captain around by his arm.

Captain Sears recoiled in alarm and his expression turned to surprise when he realized he had Mick before him.

Mick held up a hand, panting heavily. The three other men exchanged glances as they waited for him to catch his breath.

"I heard on the radio," he said between gasps. "Bad stuff! Malcolm's men aren't coming here!"

"What!" Captain Sears exclaimed. Now it was his turn to grab Mick by the arm. "So what did you hear?"

Catching his breath, Mick stood straighter and the captain released his arm. "Malcolm sent them to surround Shady Oaks; apparently he plans to take the whole damn town hostage if we don't leave here! He plans to have another talk with you - but that flash-bang will be going off before that happens. His men are almost in position, they plan to subdue our patrols and move in if they don't hear from Malcolm within the hour."

They all looked at their watches. "We have less than five minutes," Sean said softly. "Sure looks like they're not going to hear from Malcolm."

"Don't jump to conclusions just yet," Captain Sears said with a thoughtful look. "If we can get in there and grab Malcolm before the deadline I bet we can make him talk. So, let's make him our priority. Soon as that flash-bang goes off, we're in there and we locate Malcolm as quickly as possible."

The captain turned to Scott. "Go to the edge of the trees and see if you can spot him now, then we'll know where he is without searching."

"Sean, stay with me," he said before turning toward Mick. "I need you to go back and monitor the radio again. I know you don't want to, but I need to know if there's any change of plan or if they're moving in on Shady Oaks. Don't worry about radio silence, if you hear anything important, you call Sean up."

Mick frowned, and then nodded reluctantly. "You're right, I don't like this, but I'll do what you ask. He turned to his son. "I'll call you on our usual frequency if that's okay."

Sean patted the walkie strapped to his hip before taking it out and fiddling with the dials. "I'll be ready."

As Mick was leaving, Scott trotted back and he stopped to listen. "I spotted Malcolm by that big building where we heard the zombies and he's talking to a couple of his men."

After glancing at his watch once more, Captain Sears scanned the area behind him where his men were now in position and ready to go on his command. "When you hear the explosion, that's your signal to move out. Everyone knows what to do, stick to the plan and we should be successful."

Mick felt a nudge and Scott whispered in his ear. "Dad, you need to get going, we need you to let us know what they're doing down by Shady Oaks. Don't worry, we'll be okay."

"You're right," he whispered back. As he turned once again to leave, he saw the men jump in response to the flash-bang going off. Without another look back, he put his head down and ran.

★★★★

"Look, there's a big camp over there!" Mark shouted.

"Let's stick to the plan before we go near it because I don't particularly feel like being shot at," Harry shouted back as he swung the copter toward the edge of the meadow.

He was surprised at how large the lake was; he estimated it was about the size of two football fields. The meadow formed an almost perfect circle around the water and past the meadow was the tree-lined periphery. The camp was on the opposite side, with rows of tents and buildings between the meadow and tree line.

"We'll go ahead and follow the meadow around and take a look first."

Mark kept his eyes peeled for any signs of life. As they neared the south end, he heard a loud explosion and jerked his head up. He and Harry exchanged surprised looks.

He looked down and over to his right again to see a sudden flurry of activity around the camp. Men came pouring from the trees, surging forward toward the tents and buildings.

"Must be our guys!" Mark exclaimed excitedly. "We need to figure out how we can help them!"

They were already at the south end of the meadow and Harry was beginning his turn when he saw someone near the tree line standing on a road and waving at them. He pointed toward the man.

"Do you see that guy, isn't that Mick?"

Mark turned and tilted his head to see. Harry turned slightly to give him a better view. "Yeah! That's Mick!"

Mark waved back and Harry went lower, hovering a few feet above the ground. Mick began to head toward them and as he approached, something below them caused Harry to look down. What he saw made his mouth go dry. Without taking his eyes off the sight before him, he reached over and gave Mark a hard nudge in the ribs.

"Mark! What is that? Look!"

Mark peered down at the ground and at first his brain couldn't quite catch up to what his eyes were seeing. He shook his head slowly in disbelief and when he looked back up at Harry; his face was white with shock.

Before speaking, he noticed Mick and pointed. "We have to warn him!" he shouted. "He's walking right into it!"

Harry nodded grimly and headed straight for Mick, who stopped dead in his tracks and began to back up.

"We can't go any closer because of the trees!" Harry said loudly. "What do you want to do?"

"If you can get a little bit lower, I'll jump out and find out what's going on and warn him at the same time."

With a nod, Harry swung in and after opening the door; Mark gingerly put his feet on the rail then leapt toward Mick. He would have fallen if Mick hadn't reacted and caught him almost before he touched the ground.

Mick helped him stand then gave him a good shake. Mark looked at him in surprise. Mick was clearly angry and gave him another shake.

"What in the hell were you trying to do? Kill me?"

"No, we were trying to save your life," he retorted as he stepped back from Mick. "Come here."

Mark led him toward the edge of the meadow and motioned for Harry to show him. Harry had moved up and back once Mark was off, now he slowly came back and the wash from the copter's blades revealed what was hidden in the long grass.

Mark heard Mick's sudden intake of breath as they both beheld the horror before them. There were naked zombies all over, held in place with thick leather collars and leashes staked into the ground. These weren't normal

139

zombies, either. Each one was missing the lower half of their bodies from the upper thigh down so they could only crawl. They overlapped just enough to be able to touch hands.

"Anyone going in there wouldn't be coming out," Mark shouted over the roar of copter. "That's why we came at you, to make you move back."

Mick immediately remembered the solider he'd seen crawl into the meadow and swallowed hard. "Thanks," he managed to get out around his dry throat. "You saved me from a nasty death."

As Harry once again backed away, Mark said, "We heard an explosion and saw men running toward that camp up there, what's going on?"

"They're going in to get the hostages." He glanced at the copter. "Look, I don't have time to explain it all, I need to get on the walkie and have Sean pass on a warning to not go in that meadow. In the meantime, it might be helpful if you two go back to town. The man who runs the Connor Group has sent most of his men to Shady Oaks with the idea of taking over the town. They need to be warned and there's not a minute to spare."

Mark was dismayed to hear the news and shook his head glumly. "All right, we'll be on our way." He waved Harry back and as the copter slowly approached again, he turned and held out his hand. "Good luck; hopefully we'll see each other soon."

Mick didn't like the tone in Mark's voice, but nodded and shook his hand. "Going to think positive," he said while pulling out his walkie. "Okay, got to run!" Without waiting for a reply, he spun on his heel with the walkie up to his mouth and headed for the truck with the radio.

Mark got as close to the meadow as he dared and tried not to look down as Harry edged the copter close enough for him to grab a handhold and jump on the rail. The copter tilted a bit and he quickly jerked the door open and scrambled inside.

Once firmly belted in, he heaved a huge sigh of relief. He quickly filled Harry in on his conversation with Mick and as they swung around to head back, Mark tapped Harry on the arm to get his attention.

"What do think about us buzzing the camp, maybe we can cause a little more confusion to help them out."

141

"Could be dangerous, but I'm willing to give it a try."

"Let's do it then," Mark said resolutely as he automatically tightened his seat belt.

"We'll go in low and fast then head straight back to town."

As they roared toward camp, Mark had a sinking feeling when he realized a small group of soldiers were entering the meadow. He pointed and when Harry saw what was happening, shook his head.

"We can't save everyone, Mark. I'll go over their heads then hover for a second above the meadow in front of them hoping they see what's there, but it's the best I can do."

"Okay," Mark replied sadly. He watched the men stop and fall back for a moment, but as soon as they hovered over the meadow, the men headed in their direction with raised weapons.

"We can't stay here!" Harry shouted as he gunned it and turned toward camp.

Mark watched the men enter the meadow then turned away. He didn't want to see what would happen next. Behind him he heard rapid gunfire that quickly faded away. He closed his eyes and lowered his head.

"We tried and that's all we could do," Harry said in a dismal voice. "Let's see if we can be more effective at the camp."

Mark rubbed his forehead and opened his eyes. "Maybe Mick was able to let Captain Sears know we're the good guys by now.

"Let's hope so, don't relish the idea of being shot."

They shot across the meadow and rocketed across the lake toward the camp. To their surprise, there didn't seem to be much of a fight going on.

"Wow, looks like they've pretty much rounded up everyone." Mark said with relief in his voice. As they passed over a white tent he pointed. "There's Captain Sears with Mick's boys, Sean and Scott, and it looks like they have everyone who was taken hostage with them!"

"Awesome!" Harry replied with a big grin. Before reaching the camp, he swung to the right. "I don't think we need to do a flyover and possibly take fire, let's head back."

"Sounds good to me," Mark replied. As they passed the large wooden building on the end, he looked down. What he didn't realize was that he was looking at Malcolm, who was on the verge of

143

releasing all two hundred and
thirty one zombies jammed tightly
inside.

Chapter 13

Charlie stood with the others grinning like an idiot at his friends. Everything happened as he'd hoped, although it didn't go quite as he envisioned.

As soon as he tossed the flash-bang, Charlie grabbed Jenny and Brooke by the hand and pulled them to the floor. They were able to cover their ears and close their eyes right before the blinding flash and explosion. The concussion stunned him temporarily, which he wasn't expecting, but he was on his feet and pulling the girls up with him before the two men guarding them had been able to even move after they fell to the ground. He yelled at them to run, which they did and he went the other way to retrieve Jake.

Charlie almost smacked into him when they both tried to go through the plastic dividing the tent at the same time. Grabbing Jake by the front of his shirt, Charlie spun around and pushed Jake in front of him and together they ran out of the tent just as several soldiers rushed past them to subdue those still inside. A few of the soldiers even waved as they went by, most of them knew the Shady Oaks and Ambrose folks.

Now everyone was milling around and talking all at once. Charlie noticed a small group of soldiers leading several of Malcolm's men into the other large tent. He watched for a moment then approached Captain Sears and tapped him lightly on the shoulder.

"Charlie! So good to see you!" Sears said with a chuckle.

"Good to see you, too," Charlie said as he returned the grin. He gestured toward the handcuffed men. "I don't see Malcolm or his bodyguard, are they being held somewhere else?"

"I have men searching for him as we speak."

Charlie sighed with relief, confident Malcolm would soon be in custody, and then smiled when a small truck pulled up with Mick and Jimmy inside. He started walking over to talk to them when the sound of gunfire erupted off to his left.

He paused and from that area, Charlie saw two soldiers running toward them with weapons drawn. The first one to reach them shouldered his weapon and addressed the captain with fear in his voice. "Sir! We got a ton of

146

zombies coming out of a building and they're headed this way!"

Captain Sears stretched to look over the man's head and frowned. The area as far as he could see was still clear, so perhaps they had enough time to try and stop them and get the hostages out.

As he shouted orders, they heard an engine rev up and a truck appeared from behind the tents. Charlie realized it was the flatbed he'd seen earlier, only now the back contained the body of Malcolm's son still in his tube, along with Malcolm and his contingent of scientists and doctors. A generator was humming in one corner to keep Connor's oxygen and other equipment going.

For a moment, everyone was caught off guard and paused to watch the truck trundle away. Charlie gritted his teeth when Malcolm had the nerve to smile and wave as they reached the trees and disappeared from view on the dirt road leading off the mountain. Malcolm managed to throw a major distraction their way so he could escape with his son.

Captain Sears began barking orders again and everyone moved faster when they heard more gunfire, this time more rapid and sustained. He walked over to Sean and Scott and grabbed each one by an arm.

"Get all these people down the road, load them in one of the trucks and get them the hell out of here!" he shouted in their faces.

The brothers nodded and turned toward their family and friends. "Follow us, stay out of the meadow, we hug the tree line!" Sean yelled as the gunfire got louder.

Charlie was certain he could hear moaning in between shots and shouting, and tried to get a quick look toward the sounds, but there were too many soldiers in the way. He felt a hand on his shoulder and looked up.

"Time to go, let's move," Scott said grimly in his ear. Charlie nodded and joined the rest of the group, which now included Mick and Jimmy again. They followed Sean as he began to jog down toward the trees. Scott took up the rear, looking almost constantly over his shoulder. As they reached the trees, he chanced one more look and immediately froze in place.

Trying to fight down panic, he turned and sprinted past Charlie and the others to whisper

something in Sean's ear. The look
on Sean's face alarmed Charlie and
as he started to look back both
brothers began to yell at them to
run.

Sean turned and ran down the
road as Scott began to hurry
everyone along. Once Charlie
passed him, he again took up his
position in the rear with rifle in
hand. Charlie wanted to see what
was happening behind them, but at
the same time was afraid to look.

Fortunately the truck wasn't
too far down the road and Sean
helped everyone up into the back
as Scott ran past them to jump in
the driver's seat. Designed to
ferry troops back and forth, this
truck was covered and had benches
for them to sit on. Sean jumped in
and pulled up the tailgate,
cautioning them to hold on as he
knelt and swung his rifle around
to point it outside.

Charlie took a quick glance
at everyone; all of them were
panting and sweating. Mick and
Jimmy were trying to calm Brooke
while Jenny and Jake sat holding
hands and talking quietly. Sean
reached outside and gave the truck
a couple of hard smacks, Scott had
already started the vehicle and
the truck lurched forward.

"Going to be a rough ride," Sean said as he turned to face them. "So hang on and sit tight."

Charlie scooted closer to Sean and asked, "What did you see back there?"

Sean threw a quick glance at the others before turning his attention to Charlie. "I saw our guys slowly retreating," he paused and swallowed. "And that's why," he said in a low voice as he pointed toward the camp.

They were in a spot on the road where the trees were sparse and what Charlie saw sent shivers down his spine. There were zombies all over the camp and halfway across the meadow, apparently they weren't bothered by the zombies tethered to the ground. He saw a few trip and fall, only to slowly get back to their feet and continue on. Sean was right, but now the soldiers were retreating at a much faster pace.

"Are we going to make it out of here?"

"Oh, we'll make it," Sean remarked with resolve in his voice. "We may have to get out and hike back to town, but we will make it."

Charlie didn't like the thought of having to walk all the way back, but he liked the thought of being surrounded by zombies even less.

"I hope so," was all he could think of to say as he watched the zombies spread out and move ever closer toward the roads.

★★★★

Cindy and Judith looked up in surprise as Mark and Harry burst through the front door with such force that it slammed into the wall, leaving a hole where the doorknob punched through.

"We have a bad situation, I'm going to ring the bell," Mark said in a rush. He waved toward Harry as he spun on his heel and raced out the door. "He'll fill you in!" he shouted over his shoulder.

As both women stared incredulously at Harry, he tried to grin, but failed miserably. He sat down on the edge of the couch next to Cindy.

"There's not much time, so I'll make this quick," he began with a shake of his head. "We ran up to the lake and found a huge camp up there; Mark tells me it's the Connor Group. By the time we got there, Captain Sears and his men had control of the camp. Before that though, we ran into

Mick and he explained to us what was happening."

"Mick! Did you say Mick was up there?" Cindy asked in amazement. Then her eyes narrowed as she looked toward her friend. "Judith, our hunch was right, they did head up there."

Harry nodded. "Charlie is with the other people who were held hostage, but they all seem to be fine."

At their relieved looks, he continued. "We were able to talk to Mick, but only for a few minutes. He warned us that most of the Connor Group is headed this way, they plan to take over Shady Oaks."

Cindy's eyes widened in amazement as she digested what he said and Judith gasped loudly.

"We need to warn everyone about what we're dealing with here!" Judith declared as she jumped up and headed for the door. "We've had drills for zombies, not for people coming after us!"

Harry held up a hand. "Wait, I have a favor to ask." As Judith hesitated he said, "Could you please find Bitsy and your son, and send them back up to the farm? I'd like to see them both safe and out of town."

"I can do that," she replied. "They're at my house putting up the eggs, I'll stop there first."

"Grab Megan and Darrell, too," Cindy said hurriedly as she stood to retrieve her pistol and Mick's shotgun. "I'll run by Rose and Dexter's to make sure they know and can pass it along."

With a curt nod, Judith turned and rushed out the door. Cindy hesitated for a second when the church bell began to ring, and then she disappeared down the hall.

Harry stood and walked over to the door, leaning against the jamb to look out. There was already a flurry of activity as people began to leave their homes and congregate around what Harry assumed was city hall and most likely the sheriff's office. A big man in a police uniform that seemed to be two sizes too small for him pushed through the crowd and started yelling orders; from Mark's description of the man he surmised he was staring at Dexter.

He turned as Cindy reappeared and thrust a rifle toward him.

"I am assuming you're familiar with firearms," she said as he examined the gun. She handed him a box of ammunition, which he slipped into a jacket pocket.

"Unfortunately, yes," he murmured as he examined the rifle. "Never did care for guns, but my father insisted that we, Bitsy's father and I, learn to hunt. Gabe took to it, but I never did enjoy the sport."

"Now you need to know how in order to survive," Cindy replied as she checked her pistol before placing it in the holster on her right hip. She shouldered Mick's shotgun and nodded toward the door.

"Let's get going."

Harry opened the door. "After you."

He was out and somehow knew where he wanted to go. In the dim recess of his mind was an image, an echo of a memory which drew him. He still retained some basic intelligence and cognitive thinking, which gave him a definite advantage. Another plus, since he was one of the test subjects given fluids, he was able to think and not be driven by need alone.

He used the power of his thoughts and emotions, such as they were, to force the others to follow him. Once he had been someone people looked up to and admired. The embroidered name tag on his white lab coat, now torn and heavily stained, once identified him as Dr. Robert Jamieson. Now tattered and half torn off, what was left of the tag simply identified him as "Rob."

After he was bitten by one of their test subjects and turned, a few of the doctors in Malcolm's employ jokingly called him Dr. Brainiac, Dr. Cerebrum, or Dr. Synapse. Cruel men, they led him around like a prize pony until they tired of their games and experiments on him. Then they tossed him in with the others and forgot he ever existed.

Not that it mattered, he didn't care about anything other than to satisfy their ever-present thirst – it was what they all wanted – it drove them on and was always foremost in their collective thoughts.

Although he wasn't as needy as the others, but he could feel the beginning pangs of thirst stir within him. He knew where to go to find what they needed, but at that moment the others were attracted like lethal magnets to the people all around them, so he relaxed and let them have their way. For now.

Chapter 14

Charlie and Mick exchanged worried glances as they moved at a snail's pace down the poor excuse for a road. Charlie knew if they didn't pick up the pace the zombies were going to cut them off.

Daylight was slowly fading, within the hour it would be dark and they needed to get off the mountain before then.

He was startled from his thoughts as Sean opened fire on two zombies standing by the side of the road. One fell straight to the ground while the other spun in a lazy circle before dropping.

"Nice shooting," he muttered.

"Thanks," Sean replied, his eyes never leaving the zombies in the meadow.

The truck suddenly came to a screeching halt, throwing Charlie into Sean and sending them both sprawling onto the truck floor. Sean had the presence of mind and the training to keep his rifle pointed up and away from them. He rolled to his side and immediately crouched back down next to the tailgate. Charlie followed his example by rolling over and he quickly took his seat again.

They heard the driver's side door open and Scott quickly dropped the tailgate. "Zombies on the road ahead, we're going on foot so we can avoid them."

Without a word, Sean jumped out and turned to help the others while Scott kept watch. Once everyone was out, Scott turned toward them.

"Stay really close, try to not make a sound, and no talking - we need to sneak past these guys if we're going to make it out," he said in a low voice. "We don't have much time until it gets dark so let's see how much distance we can put between them and us before then."

Mick stepped forward. "Do you think we should chance a walkie call to your Mom? Let them know what's going on here?"

"Dad, I'd love to, but we can't," Scott said with a shake of his head. "If Malcolm's men hear our conversation, they'll know we're on to them and that could cause them to attack the town sooner. We want our people ready and waiting for them so they lose the element of surprise."

"Gotcha," Mick said forlornly. He didn't want to admit it, but he needed to hear Cindy's voice, wanted to hear her say everything would work out.

"Okay, line up in this order - Brooke, Jimmy, Dad, Jenny, Jake, and Charlie - with Sean at the rear," Scott said as he maneuvered them around like they were puppets on a string. Once they were lined up he grinned. "Do you feel like you're in grade school again? Sorry 'bout that, but there's a method to my madness. Okay, let's go."

Scott turned and began to walk quickly down through the trees and Mick realized that with a little luck they should come out right by the pickup. Taking a chance, he scurried up to his son.

"I know you said to stay in place and no talking, but if we keep going this way we'll run into the pickup and we can take it out of here," he said in a loud whisper as he tried to match his son's stride through the woods.

"Awesome," Scott replied. "Will try to head right for it then, now you better get back in line before Sean decides he needs to come up here and find out what's going on."

"All right," Mick huffed and slowed his stride until he could fall in behind Jimmy.

159

He got back into step with the group and they hurried through the trees for several seconds before they heard gunfire and shouting directly off to their right.

Mick turned his head toward the sound and didn't see Scott slow down and hold up a hand. He plowed right into Jimmy, almost knocking them both to the ground.

"Oh wow, so sorry," he whispered, clutching Jimmy by the arm to steady him.

Scott turned and trotted past them to confer with his brother again. After a few words were exchanged he motioned for everyone to join them. Once huddled together, Scott nodded in the direction where shots were still going off.

"I think we've got a problem," he began in a loud whisper. He looked up over Jimmy's head to make sure they were safe before continuing.

"We don't know where the zombies are now and we're almost in total darkness until the moon comes up. Sean and I think it best if we go on our own. We haven't gone too far off the road, so we will drive up here then come and get you."

"Where do you suggest we go?" Charlie asked in a low voice. "I don't see any place that we would be safe."

"Well, there is one place," Sean murmured. He slowly raised his gun and pointed it in the air. "Up there."

Mick looked up with the others and heard Brooke groan.

"We don't have a lot of time, so let's do this. Ladies first," Scott said as he walked over to the nearest tree, a nice oak with plenty of branches for them to sit on. He put his hands together to give everyone a boost and being scared of what was around them, it took less than a few minutes to have everyone in the tree.

When Mick looked down at his sons and saw them grinning up at them, he wagged a finger. "I know what you're thinking so don't even go there."

Sean played innocent, opening his eyes wide and holding out his hands. "Hey, we weren't thinking that you all look like a pack of monkeys up there!"

Scott snorted and shook his head and he moved away from the tree. "C'mon, we need to see what's going on," he growled at his brother.

161

Sean waved at them. "Be quiet up there and no moving around, we don't want those things spotting you," he said before turning to join his brother.

"Be careful!" Mick hissed. Sean waved again without turning around.

Mick watched them talk again for a second before they separated and began to use the trees for cover as they went in different directions. He could see them dart here and there until the forest eventually blocked his view.

He was always amazed at how they could operate without even communicating; they always seemed to know where their twin was. When they were younger, they loved to play paintball and they almost always decimated their competition.

Mick heard a branch crack and looked up in time to see Brooke easing down to another branch right above him. He held out a hand to help steady her and she gave him a small, nervous smile in return.

"Dad, I'm scared," she said in a shaky voice.

He patted her hand reassuringly as he glanced around them again. He was about to reply when gunfire erupted once more, only it was much closer this time and he could hear men yelling to each other.

Mick initially felt foolish for having to hide up in a tree, but now he wondered if they should go even higher, a low stray bullet could hit one of them while they were sitting on the lower branches. He waved at Charlie who was sitting almost directly opposite of him on the other side of the tree trunk.

Charlie saw him immediately and waved back. Mick leaned forward so his whisper would carry further. "I think we need to go higher, the way they're shooting down there we could get hit."

Charlie nodded and slowly made his way to his feet. He tapped first Jenny and then Jake on a foot and pointed up. Fortunately they both immediately understood what he wanted and began to slowly make their way up the tree.

Mick turned to Brooke. "We need to get higher, get Jimmy to give you a hand up."

Brooke nodded and turned toward Jimmy. Tugging on his jeans to get his attention, she held her hand up to him when he looked down. "Dad says we need to go higher," she said in a loud whisper.

Jimmy bent down and grasped her hand to pull her up. She placed her right foot on a higher branch and began to pull herself up with Jimmy's help. Shots rang out even closer, causing her to jump in fear.

Mick watched in horror as her foot slipped off the branch and she reflexively jerked on Jimmy's arm for support. Together, they both lost their balance and slid past the branches before free falling to the ground below, Jimmy falling headfirst.

Mick heard Jenny gasp and everyone froze for a moment before scrambling down. Brooke seemed to be uninjured and crawled over to Jimmy, tears streaming down her face as she stroked his cheek and frantically whispered his name over and over.

Mick dropped down beside her and as he put an arm around her, Jake knelt down to check Jimmy. They all watched as he worked swiftly; first he checked for a pulse then ran his hands up and down Jimmy's arms and legs. He looked up at them.

"I'm going to try and wake him so I can determine if he has a neck or spine injury before we move him. If I can't wake him up we'll have to chance it because we sure can't stay here."

"This is all my fault," Brooke sobbed into Mick's shoulder. "If I had been braver and not such a baby we wouldn't have fallen."

Mick gave her a reassuring hug. "You slipped, it was an accident and I think you've been plenty brave. Most people would have run screaming into the woods after experiencing what you've been through."

Jake made a fist and with moderate pressure gave the young man a sternal rub; he called his name and rubbed his fist into Jimmy's chest again.

"What's he doing?" Brooke asked as she wiped her eyes with the back of her hand.

Jenny, who was sitting on her haunches on the other side of Brooke, leaned over and whispered. "He's trying to get him to wake up, what he's doing is painful, but won't hurt Jimmy."

To everyone's relief, Jimmy's eyelids fluttered and he gave a low moan of pain. Jake placed a hand on his forehead to keep him from moving.

"Jimmy, do you have any pain in your neck?"

Jimmy's eyes opened and he was silent for a moment as he looked at everyone clustered around. "Umm, no pain there, but my butt hurts."

Everyone grinned and Jake chuckled as he slowly turned Jimmy on his side. After a quick exam he stood and motioned toward Charlie.

"Help me get him up."

Slowly they stood Jimmy up and held him there for a moment. When he tried to take a step he gasped in pain and grimaced.

Jake frowned. "I think you may have done some damage to your tail bone," he said while reaching down to grab his backpack. "But we don't have time to stand around here anymore."

He nodded at Mick. "Can you and Charlie help him? I think we should get moving."

"Sure thing," Mick said as he gave Brooke a quick hug and releasing her, stood and hurried over to put a steadying arm around Jimmy. Jenny and Brooke got to their feet and after shouldering their bags, stood together.

Jenny asked in a low voice, still mindful of what surrounded them, "So where do we go?"

"The only thing I can think of is we go back to camp. We can tell by the gunfire and other noise that those things are moving off, it might actually be the safest place around here now."

Mick thought for a moment and nodded. "You've got a point, I sure don't want to try and make it down the mountain with those things crawling all over."

"Not to mention possibly getting shot by accident," Charlie hissed. He nodded toward the camp. "Let's get going."

They slowly moved out, moving from one tree to another and mindful to stay away from the meadow as they made their way back.

As gunfire and shouts erupted again, Mick mentally crossed his fingers and hoped they would make if back safely. His thoughts turned to his sons; they would have to find some way to let them know their plan was changed, if he needed to break radio silence he would. There was no way he would let Sean and Scott drive unaware into a group of zombies with armed soldiers right behind them.

Shaking his head, he tightened his grip on Jimmy and tried to focus on the task at hand.

****

They were on the move, which was exactly what he wanted. All he had to do was think the thing, and it was done. When he was still alive, he and his peers found it amazing how the zombie brain had changed. No longer burdened with rational thought and other cognitive functions, a form of mass telepathy emerged based on need, and their only need was to satisfy the thirst.

For a long time most of them wandered around in small groups, but once they were brought together by the Connor Group, he emerged as leader. He was the strongest and as they moved toward their destination, he could feel others off in the distance. With a single thought, he called to them and felt them respond. By the time they reached their destination they would be almost unstoppable. Then they would quench their thirst again and again – and again.

Chapter 15

Cindy turned to Judith as Rose closed the shelter door and secured it. "Well, that takes care of all the kids and everyone who can't fight. Guess we should get over to the hardware store and get in position."

They both trotted down the hall and up the stairs where Harry was waiting for them. As they approached, he waved a walkie talkie in the air. "We're all set with these, use channel four."

Judith nodded and pulling it out of her backpack, fiddled with the dial. Cindy patted hers, which was clipped to her belt. "I'm going to be with Judith, so I'm leaving my settings where they are so either the twins or Mick can contact us if they ever break radio silence."

Harry turned and opened the door that led outside. Cindy peered over his shoulder at the apartment building across the street. Once again a meeting place, Dexter was doing what he did best, bellowing orders for everyone to find their places and get ready for an imminent attack.

"Guess I'll be leaving you ladies for now, I'm meeting Mark

169

at the chopper, and we're going to move it to the McKenzie farm."

"You better get going," Cindy said with a smile as she gave him a nudge out the door. "We definitely don't want the Connor Group to get their hands on a helicopter, which would be a bad deal all the way around."

"Agree," Harry said solemnly. He gave them a quick wave as he turned to go. "See you soon!"

Judith followed Cindy out the door and they walked together along the back of the building then made a sharp left until they were at the street. They jogged the rest of the way down to the hardware store where they quickly made their way up the stairs to stand watch over their section of the street.

Judith rummaged around in her backpack and brought out the walkie again, carefully placing it on a windowsill and checking to make sure it was on the proper channel. Then she pulled out a large thermos and a paper bag.

"Coffee and homemade donuts," she said with a grin. "I come prepared."

Cindy chuckled. "Indeed you do, think I could use a cup right now."

Judith pulled a large metal mug out of her bag and waggled her eyebrows at Cindy, causing both women to laugh.

Cindy gratefully accepted the mug full of hot coffee and gingerly sipped. "Ah, that hits the spot!" she said with a happy sigh.

"Sorry it's black, I know you like cream and sugar, but I figured we could be here awhile and it would help keep us awake."

"No, it's fine," Cindy said agreeably, taking another sip.

Both women jumped and Cindy almost dropped her mug when Judith's walkie crackled to life. Both women listened quietly as the groups patrolling the town checked in. Once it grew quiet again, Cindy realized she was holding her breath and let it out in a whoosh.

"They all checked in," Judith pointed out as she filled her own mug and took a drink. She made a face and set it down on a nearby counter. "I hate coffee, give me tea anytime," she said with a chuckle.

Cindy nodded toward the window. "I hope this turns out to be nothing, it's getting dark and that will make it hard to see anything."

"Well, we do have one set of night vision goggles, courtesy of Lilly," Judith said as she bent down to retrieve her bag and pull them out.

"What else do you have in there?" Cindy said with a laugh.

"You'd be surprised," her friend quipped with a wink and a finger to her lips. "But it's a secret."

Cindy grinned and shook her head. She glanced out the window and turned away, only to jerk her gaze back toward the window again. "I think I just saw something."

Judith followed her gaze and stared out the window. They watched silently for several seconds before Cindy shook her head.

"Guess it was nothing..."

Judith stopped her by reaching out and grabbing her arm. "No, I see something - look over by the park!"

Cindy squinted, shadows were lengthening in the growing darkness and it was becoming difficult to make out anything. Then she saw it - something very dark and large was moving slowly down the street toward them.

"I think it's an SUV," Judith said nervously. She tucked a strand of curly blond hair behind an ear. She reached out and picked up the walkie.

"Wouldn't someone have called out if they were headed in?"

Cindy nodded, her eyes still fastened on the vehicle. "Yeah, they're supposed to."

"Dexter, come in," Judith said carefully into the walkie.

"I'm here," Dexter said in his gravely voice.

"Cindy and I are in position at the hardware store and there's an SUV coming slowly down the street. Do you know if anyone is out moving around?"

"Lemme check."

They both waited as Dexter roared out over the walkie to anyone moving in town to let him know pronto. Cindy shook her head as Judith rolled her eyes.

"Some things never change," Cindy said dryly. She bent down, fished around in her own backpack, and pulled out binoculars. Walking over to another window further down, she held them up and focused them.

"What are you trying to do?"

"I know the windows are tinted and it's still at the end of the street, but I'd like to see if I can catch any glimpse of who is in there before it's too dark to see."

173

"Gotcha," Judith replied. She started to turn away and go into the next room to take a look when Cindy held out a hand.

"Judith! Come look!" she hissed as she waved her hand frantically. "They've stopped!"

Judith hurried over to peer over Cindy's shoulder. They both gasped when several men in dark clothing exited from the vehicle and ran to their side of the street to take cover by the buildings. Both women knew immediately these were not people from Shady Oaks.

"Oh, this is not good," Judith said in a low voice. Still watching the street, she quickly called Dexter on the walkie.

"Dex! This SUV we're watching is not from here, about six men piled out and they're somewhere down the street!"

The walkie was silent for a moment. Cindy and Judith stared at each other until Dexter's voice came through again.

"Okay, you two hold your position and stay out of sight, we're on our way."

"Roger that," Judith said softly. She released the talk button and sighed loudly as she looked around the room. Shadows were lengthening and it was getting hard to see. "Guess we should hunker down by the windows and keep watch until they get here."

Cindy grabbed a nearby folding chair and sat near the window, her binoculars around her neck. Judith watched Cindy check her pistol before placing it on her lap.

Judith slid another chair over to her window, she had the night vision goggles in hand and the shotgun Cindy brought along was at her feet. Like Cindy, she was more comfortable with a pistol, but there had been no time to fetch hers, so now she had to use Mick's shotgun.

They sat silently, looking out the windows for almost half an hour before Cindy spoke softly in the dark room.

"I always thought that if anything happened, I'd have Mick by my side and that kept me from being afraid. Without him here, I'm really scared...I wish he and Charlie had stayed in town and were here with us now."

Judith leaned over and patted her friend's hand. "No reason to be scared, Dexter is coming with help, it will be all right."

"I hope so," Cindy murmured in a shaky voice. She suddenly sat

up straighter when sudden movement
from the park across the street
caught her eye.

"I think I see them now. Look
across the street."

As Judith turned to the
window, gunfire and the resulting
flashes erupted on the street
below them. She heard Cindy gasp
as she reached down for the
shotgun.

"Can I be scared now?"

"Yeah," Judith muttered
grimly as she released the safety
and heard Cindy do the same with
her pistol. "Now we can both be
scared."

★★★★

"I can't believe we made it
back in one piece," Mick grunted
as he helped deposit Jimmy onto
the nearest cot. He had sweat
dripping from his face and wiped
it off as best he could with the
back of his shirt sleeve.

Even with Jimmy in tow, they
managed a slow trot almost the
entire way back to camp and
everyone needed a few moments to
catch their breath.

Mick watched Jake disappear
toward the back, muttering
something about finding medical
supplies. Charlie and Jenny were
busy trying to secure the flaps to

the tent so no zombie stragglers could easily get in, although the place appeared to be completely deserted.

Brooke found a chair and sat next to Jimmy, worry etched on her face. Mick decided to see if he could help Jake and found the doctor shining a flashlight into a cabinet drawer as he dug through the contents.

"Anything I can do to help?"

Jake looked up. "Sure, we need to take all this medicine back with us so see if you can find a couple of good size boxes; we can really use almost everything here." He picked up a bottle and gave it a shake. "I found some muscle relaxers, these should help Jimmy."

Mick held out a hand. "If you want, I'll take those up front while I'm looking for boxes."

"That'll work, thanks," Jake said distractedly. He straightened up and surveyed the area. "I can't believe they left so much behind, but it's great for us and especially good for my research. After I provided some of my information, they were in the final stages of synthesizing a new vaccine and if they left enough behind, I should be able to continue that work or at least see if they were able to fix their deadly problem."

Mick found a small battery-operated lantern and turned it on. He glanced around the room and was surprised to see how much equipment Malcolm left behind. He surmised that Malcolm was planning to come back and soon. His gaze fell on a large box in the corner.

"From the look of things, you may get your wish," he said as he retrieved the box and handed it to Jake.

"I hope so; if we can keep any more people from dying then we may all have a chance to have real lives again."

As he helped fill the box with medical supplies, Mick's thoughts turned to his sons. Brooke had the idea to leave a note on the tree, which they did and he knew they would see it when they returned. Lucky for them that Jake always carried paper and pens with him; he never knew when some idea would come to mind that he didn't want to forget.

"When do you think Sean and Scott will get here?"

Jake shrugged as he turned to pick up another box of what looked like syringes. "Well, let's say they've already made it to the truck and managed to get back up

178

here. Then they would have gone on foot the rest of the way to the tree and found the note. They would drive both trucks back to the camp. So, I'm guessing they should be here in about fifteen or twenty minutes."

"Then we should probably hurry with this stuff," Mick huffed as he placed another box by the entrance.

They worked silently for several minutes before Mick stopped and looked around. "We could really use a dolly; think I'll see if I can find one."

"Good idea," Jake murmured while scanning various vials and tubes inside a small refrigerator. He turned toward Mick with a large smile on his face. He held up a small wire basket full of capped tubes.

"Look at this! They left a batch of the vaccine behind; I can't wait to examine one of these!"

Mick smiled back. "That's great news! If it works then all we need to do is replicate what's in there, right?"

Jake carefully placed the basket back into the fridge and closed the door. "Perhaps. I don't know if this is new or just

179

another batch of the current vaccine."

Mick watched Jake pick up a large red and white cooler and return to the fridge to pack his precious cargo. "Okay, I'm going to find more boxes and a dolly or hand cart or anything with wheels to help us haul this stuff outside. Soon as Sean and Scott get here, we can load up and get back to Shady Oaks."

He didn't have a flashlight and the lantern he left behind with Jake cast such a dim light that when he walked through the plastic barrier he almost ran into Charlie.

"You two need any help? The boys just pulled up, Jenny's out there talking to them."

"They did? That's great!" Mick said with a wide grin. "Looking for boxes and a dolly, want to help?"

"Sure," Charlie said as he turned to follow Mick back toward the entrance. "There are boxes up front, and I haven't seen a dolly, but I'll look around."

"Sounds good, I'll get the boys to come help us load stuff and take a quick look outside while I'm at it."

He stopped for a moment by the cot Jimmy was now sitting on,

with Brooke still by his side. Two
large lanterns they found did a
surprisingly good job of lighting
the space and he could clearly see
both of them. He tossed the small
package of muscle relaxers into
Jimmy's lap.

"Feeling better?"

Jimmy gave him a small smile
and nodded. "Yeah, it doesn't hurt
as much now. Jake thinks I bruised
my tail bone."

He looked toward his
daughter. "Boys are here, we're
going to need some help loading
supplies Jake needs, think you can
tear yourself away for a little
bit to give us a hand?"

Brooke patted Jimmy's hand
and jumped up. "Sure, now that I
know Jimmy is feeling better, I'd
be glad to."

Mick gave her a quick hug.
"Okay Missy, go in the back and
Jake will get you started."

"Going!" she said with a
giggle and a small wave.

They both watched until she
disappeared behind the plastic
curtain. Mick turned to Jimmy.

"I see you have some water;
Jake said to take two of those. Do
you need anything else before I
head outside?"

"No, I'm good."

Mick gave him a grin. "Well, take it easy and when we finish loading the supplies we'll be back to help you get out to the truck."

Jimmy nodded and began removing the tablets from their foil pack. Mick hurried over to the entrance and grabbed his bag. He quickly pulled out his flashlight and turned it on as he rushed outside, he was eager to touch base with his sons. He didn't like being stuck in Malcolm's camp when everyone in Shady Oaks was in danger. Once again he felt guilty for sneaking off with Charlie.

"Uh oh," he said softly, slowing down as the beam from his flashlight caught the worried looks on Sean's and Scott's faces. Jenny was standing next to them and her expression mirrored theirs. Mick sighed. Whatever news they had obviously wasn't good and he felt his heart sink down to his shoes.

★★★★

He began to draw them back, they were becoming too scattered as they chased their very elusive prey. He felt a sense of urgency and tightened his focus and control. Slowly, they began to respond. He closed his eyes and waited. They gathered around him and when their minds quieted, he opened his eyes. He threw out an image to keep them centered on him and as he went forward, they obediently fell in behind.

He was learning, so as they continued on their journey he occasionally threw them an image of feeding, which kept them moving ever closer to the town below.

Chapter 16

"Where is Dexter?" Judith hissed impatiently. She cautiously peered over the window sill. After several seconds, she slowly sat back down and fiddled with the dial on her walkie.

Cindy watched her friend for a moment then closed her eyes, her thoughts drifting toward Mick and what he might be doing at that moment. She knew she should be angry with him, but his heart was in the right place and he was only trying to help.

Both women immediately tensed when they heard the wooden stairs leading up to their floor creak. Cindy let out a sigh of relief when, even in the darkness, she recognized the bulky shape of Dexter as he stepped onto the landing. He carried a flashlight and it briefly flickered on each woman's face. He turned it off and strode over to Judith's window to look outside.

"We have at least four suspicious vehicles in various places around town," he said softly while still peering out the window. In the full darkness it was nearly impossible to see anything since they didn't have the luxury of street lights for the time being. "We have them covered and so far nothing is moving, except for the men you saw earlier."

"We don't know where they went," Cindy said as she stood up and stretched. "My best guess is they're hiding somewhere on this side of the street in one of the buildings further down."

"Well, I'm going back down where my men are waiting. We'll flush them out, so don't you two worry. Sit tight and I'll send someone up to let you know when it's safe to come down."

Cindy frowned. They all knew how large and well trained the Connor Group was, and it seemed to her that Dexter was taking the situation far too lightly.

"Please be careful, sounds like they're just scouting the area. We have no idea where their main force is located. For all we know these vehicles could be diversions."

"True, I've taken that into consideration. We should be able to handle anything they throw at us now that everyone's in position. They've lost their advantage and that should make them think twice about attacking or at least get them to rethink their plan, which will give us even more time to strengthen our defenses, such as they are."

Cindy digested Dexter's remarks for a moment before nodding slowly in agreement. "I'm hoping they decide it's not worth the fight and move on out."

"Okay, I'm out of here for now," Dexter said with a grunt as he pushed himself away from the window and headed back toward the stairs. "If you see anything, let us know."

"Will do," said Judith. She was still straining to see out the window and didn't turn to watch him leave. She glanced at Cindy. "I hope this whole situation can be resolved peacefully."

Cindy was about to respond in the affirmative when they both jumped at the sound of rapid arms fire close by. She cast a baleful glance at her friend as someone below in the street returned fire.

"Well, don't think that's gonna happen," she murmured grimly, her eyes full of fear. She gripped her gun tightly and took a deep breath to steady herself. Once again she wished Mick were at her side.

Everything was eerily quiet for several minutes when directly below them, they heard glass breaking as the door to the hardware store was kicked open. Without speaking, both women quietly readied their weapons as they listened to what sounded like several people moving around and talking below.

Cindy felt her heart race as they both focused all their attention on the stairs. Please don't let them come up here, she prayed silently. She wasn't sure when it came right down to it that she could actually take another person's life, or even be able to pull the trigger, and she didn't want to find out.

"Please," she whispered under her breath when she heard footsteps approaching the stairs. More gunfire erupted below.

"Please," she whispered again as she brought up her gun with shaking hands and took aim in the direction of the stairs.

"Please."

****

"Let's go inside the tent so we can talk to everyone," Scott said. He gave his father a troubled look as they followed Sean and Jenny inside. Within moments they were all assembled. Their serious demeanor scared Mick more than anything and he was sure what they had to say wasn't going to ease his fears.

"Right before we got to Charlie's truck we ran into Captain Sears, they were regrouping and planning to head into Shady Oaks to take on Malcolm's men. They went with us to the truck and on the way he told us that right in the middle of fighting the zombies, they all seemed to disappear into the forest."

"Yep," Sean interjected with a nod. "One minute they were almost overrun and the next – not a zombie in sight. No one has any idea where they went or where they're headed."

"Anyway," Scott continued with a glance at his brother. "They were regrouping when we ran into them, they should be on their way to Shady Oaks by now to help out. Captain Sears told us he'd sent a few scouts ahead to assess the situation and it doesn't look good. They reported that Malcolm's men have taken up positions outside of Shady Oaks and they watched a few vehicles beginning to infiltrate and put men on the ground."

Mick rubbed the scar on his cheek nervously. "So are you saying the attack has begun?"

Scott nodded grimly. "Sounds like it. We're hoping everyone in Shady Oaks was ready for them and can hold them off until the troops get there. We really need to get everything and everyone loaded up so we can get down there to help out."

"Well, let's get to it then," Charlie said as he got up from the stool he'd been sitting on.

Without another word everyone got busy and within ten minutes they had all the supplies piled into the back of both trucks. Charlie, Jenny, and Jake were sandwiched in between boxes, with more boxes on their laps in the big truck. Brooke waited outside Charlie's truck as Mick and Sean carefully helped Jimmy into the back seat. Scott already had the truck running and in gear.

Mick turned to Brooke. "Hop in," he said with a grin as he held a hand out to her. Returning the grin she took his hand, but suddenly jerked back and away with a shriek.

Mick watched in surprise as she fell to the ground and began to scoot backward, still shrieking. She was looking down at her feet and as his gaze followed hers, he froze in place and felt his mouth go dry.

Like a dog reluctant to give up a favorite bone, somehow one of the collared zombies from the meadow was loose, and now dug its filthy and ragged claws into her ankle. The wretched and naked creature, which was once a woman, was trying to pull itself up her leg to bite her, jaws snapping rapidly.

Mick stared in horror and before he could react, Sean calmly stepped over and grabbing it by the collar, jerked it off his sister and flung it toward the front of the truck.

Mick hurried over to help Brooke and grimaced when he saw her left ankle. There were several long and deep scratches running almost up to her knee, and he knew from the experience they had with the former mayor of Shady Oaks, that this injury could be a death sentence.

He was barely aware of Sean walking over to get something from Scott. As he crouched down next to a sobbing and shaking Brooke, he saw Sean flip the zombie over as it was trying to crawl away and pin it to the ground. He drove the metal spike in his hand right through the its bald and rotting skull. As he pulled the spike out, he leaned forward and frowned.

Sean motioned for his brother. "You gotta see this," he said with a shake of his head. Scott jumped out of the truck and together the brothers took a good look. After a brief discussion, Scott walked back to the truck and reaching in, turned off the ignition.

"I think we should take her back inside so I can get a good look at those scratches," Jake said in Mick's ear.

Mick nodded and together they helped Brooke up and hurried her inside. Jenny followed with a flashlight and grabbed a nearby lantern. She handed it to Mick, who placed it on the stool Charlie sat on earlier.

Mick knew the fear in his daughter's face mirrored his own and he took a deep breath to steady himself. He gave her a small, but what he hoped was an encouraging smile as he helped her to sit down on the cot.

"Don't worry," he said as he smoothed her hair back from her face. Jenny handed her a box of tissue and patted her hand before heading outside. "Jake will get those scratches cleaned up and you'll be fine."

"I wish Mom was here," Brooke said in a scared, little-girl voice.

Mick winced. Cindy would probably never forgive him for this, and he deserved whatever wrath she threw his way, but he wished she was with them, too.

Jake thoroughly cleaned the scratches and after applying a thick salve of antibiotic ointment, wrapped gauze around the wounds. Jenny returned with Jimmy and helped him sit next to Brooke. Jake stood and faced Mick.

"Let's talk," he said with a nod of his head toward the entrance. Mick followed him outside. Jake walked about fifty feet and stopped. Turning toward Mick, he frowned.

"I'm not going to mince words, we don't have time for that," he said in a low voice. He ran a hand through his hair and shook his head. "Brooke is probably infected from the scratches and we both know what can happen."

Mick didn't want to hear what Jake was saying, but he nodded bleakly.

Jake continued, now looking down at the ground and dragging the toe of his tennis shoe in the dirt. "We do have an option, though." He looked up at Mick again, then glanced past him and nodded.

Mick turned to see his sons approaching, concern etched on both their faces.

"I was about to explain to your dad what options we may have in regard to helping Brooke. I believe that Malcolm's scientists and doctors finally perfected a cure for this disease and I do believe I have a few vials of that cure. However, I can't be sure it will work because I'm certain they had no time to run tests. If we do nothing, Brooke will die and turn, we all know that. What I want to suggest is that we don't put her in a coma like they did with Connor, but to sedate her instead to relax her and slow her system down, which should buy her more time until we're absolutely certain we have an effective cure. We have everything we need right here to do what needs to be done."

Mick thought over what Jake told them. He felt more hopeful than before, at least there was a good chance Brooke could be saved.

"Brooke is young and healthy and although nothing is for certain, I'm very optimistic about a very favorable outcome if we indeed do have the cure."

"I can see the sense in everything you're saying," Mick said slowly. He felt sick to his stomach. "I'm not sure it's such a good idea to stay here though, what if the zombies come back? Or Malcolm? I'm sure they were planning on returning for all of this, there's no way he'd abandon everything now that he's so close to getting his son back."

"With everything that's going on down at Shady Oaks, this is probably the safest place to be right now," Scott said. He waved his flashlight around where they were standing. "Sean and I will stand watch. Those tethered zombies had their vocal chords cut so they couldn't make noise and there's no telling how many more may be loose and crawling around. We'll have the trucks ready to go at a moment's notice, too."

"The sooner we get started, the better it will be for Brooke,"

Jake interjected. He looked at Mick. "Well, what do you say?"

Mick bit the bottom of his lip before nodding. "Guess we'd better get back in there and explain to her what needs to happen."

With a heavy heart, Mick led the way back in to the tent, his mind racing on how he was going to explain everything to his very scared daughter.

****

They were on their way, finally. Although stronger than most of them it still took all his concentration, such as it was, to corral the others. When thirst was their driving force, it was sometimes difficult to get through to them.

There were times when he had trouble himself staying focused as the thirst in him became stronger. He didn't know how long it had been since the fluids were delivered intravenously through an artery in his neck, all he knew was that his thirst was slowly increasing, which in turn weakened his ability to control the others. He knew what they needed and in his muddled mind, he remembered where they had a good chance of finding satisfaction.

If he could keep them together long enough, they would soon come to a place where all of them could find relief, even if temporary, from the raging thirst inside.

He shared this image with the others, which spurred them eagerly toward their destination. Along the way, they picked up stragglers wandering aimlessly through the woods, slowly increasing their numbers. Almost three hundred strong, they steadily drew closer to their destination.

Chapter 17

Cindy took a deep breath and stole a fearful glance at Judith, who quickly hurried over to her side.

"C'mon!" she hissed under her breath as she grabbed Cindy by the elbow. "Let's get out of here before they come up, there's a set of stairs in the next room, they come out on the back porch."

Cindy silently followed close behind as they crept quickly into the next room. Judith eased a door open and looked down, with Cindy peering over her shoulder. Judith flicked on her flashlight and revealed a set of tiny and very narrow wooden stairs descending into the darkness below.

"I didn't realize these were here," Cindy whispered as she turned on her own flashlight and quickly descended behind her friend. Judith paused on the last step and cautiously peered around the door jamb.

"It's clear, let's get the hell out of here," she whispered as she turned toward Cindy. "I think we should head for the apartments, someone will be there and we can let them know what's going on here. We sure don't want to use the walkies right now."

"Okay," Cindy whispered back. She aimed her flashlight toward the ground. "Right behind you."

Judith scurried toward the back door and quietly turned the lock on the door then slid the dead bolt open with a faint click.

They both hurried out and trotted across the street and down the road until they reached the apartments. To her surprise, it seemed as though no one was around. Ever since the first day Shady Oaks was reclaimed, someone was always there.

Cindy remembered when they first arrived in Shady Oaks, it was the first place they stayed and it seemed as though everyone went through a short stay at the apartments first before settling into a home. Now it seemed totally deserted and the only sound she heard was her own rapid breathing.

"I'm going to check inside," Judith whispered and without waiting for a reply trotted over to the door and disappeared from view.

Cindy followed and lingered outside the door, alert for any sound or movement. Judith reappeared a few moments later, followed by an elderly man Cindy recognized as Casey McMillan. According to Dexter and Charlie, Casey and his friend Barry did a lot to help get Shady Oaks up and running again. Cindy often saw him doing odd jobs and although they always exchanged friendly nods when seeing each other, she had never actually spoken to him. Judith had known him for years and after quick introductions, she turned to Cindy.

"Casey here says there was a skirmish along the main road and everyone not assigned a post high tailed it over there," Judith said as she flicked her flashlight back on. "I think we should go get the truck and find Dexter, most likely he'll be somewhere near the main road. We definitely need to let him know about the people in the store and see what he wants to do."

"I'm supposed to stay here and keep an eye on things," Casey interjected. He cocked his head to the left and grinned at them. "But I'm thinkin' you need to get to Dexter right now so let's take my truck, it will save you time." He nodded toward a small, beat up red truck sitting alone in the small parking area.

"Thanks, and you're right, we should hurry," Cindy replied with a smile as she holstered the pistol.

"I'll ride in the back so you two can get better acquainted," Judith said as she turned and headed toward the truck.

They quickly got settled in the truck and as it rumbled to life, Casey glanced at Cindy as he threw the truck into gear and headed for the street. "I've heard a lot about you and your family, you should be proud."

"I am, and thank you. I've also heard good things about you, too."

Casey turned onto the street and to Cindy's surprise, stomped on the accelerator, causing her to grab for support as she fell back into her seat. She heard a muffled yelp from behind and turned to see Judith righting herself in the truck bed. After Judith grinned and gave her a thumb up, she chuckled and turned back to Casey.

He was looking in the rear view mirror and Cindy chuckled again at the look on his face. "Sorry!" he yelled at Judith. "Sometimes I have a bit of a lead foot," he said contritely to

Cindy. "I want to get us there, but I'll take it a little slower."

"I think we'd appreciate that," Cindy said lightly. She patted him on the shoulder and could feel he was not much more than skin and bones. She'd definitely have to invite him over for a few dinners. "But yeah, we should probably try to get there in one piece."

He glanced at her again and winked. Her eyes widened and when he laughed out loud, she joined in. She was beginning to like this feisty old man and was sorry she hadn't met him sooner. She decided then and there that when everything settled down, she would make it a point to get to know as many people in town as she could.

"I'm taking the side streets and coming up from behind," Casey said as he took another turn. His headlights lit up still-deserted homes as they swung by and headed toward the main road into town.

"Someone needs to head back over here and mow those yards," he remarked. "High grass just begs for rats and other vermin to come investigate."

Before Cindy could respond, she heard a strange noise. Suddenly the whole windshield shattered and she realized someone was shooting at them. They both automatically ducked.

"Turn on the next side street!" Cindy yelled, pointing. She turned to see Judith lying on her side in the back, eyes wide with fright.

"Don't have to tell me twice," Casey yelled back. Fortunately, the next street appeared quickly and he jerked the wheel hard to the right.

As he accelerated, Cindy turned back and pointed to a small stand of pine trees. "I think we'd better stop, so why don't you pull in over there?"

Casey nodded and flicked off his headlights before reaching the trees. He turned into a neighboring driveway and drove across the yard right into the center of the trees, then turned off the engine. Cindy opened her door and Judith immediately jumped in.

"Well, wasn't expecting that," she said in a shaky voice. She rubbed her arms vigorously. "Scared me to death."

"These Connor people must be everywhere," Cindy said as she tucked a stray strand of hair behind her ear with a shaky hand.

202

"I think we should go on foot from here, it's not that far and we will probably be safer if we're not such a big target."

No sooner had she spoken than a flash of light behind them briefly lit up the truck. Within seconds, they were making their way carefully down a ditch about eight feet deep with steeply slanted sides that ran along the other side of the trees.

Judith had Casey by the arm to help him and Cindy reached the bottom of the ditch first. The night was turning cooler and damp, Cindy could see a light mist beginning to form off to her right. For a moment she allowed herself to think of Mick and wondered if he was doing better than they were. Once Judith and Casey were beside her, they turned and silently walked single file down the middle of the ditch, occasionally dodging small puddles of water. Cindy hoped they were walking away from the danger behind them and toward the safety Dexter and the rest of their friends offered.

****

Brooke took the two small blue pills Jake offered her and

with a small smile, put them in her mouth and washed them down with several small sips of water. She handed the glass to Jake, who passed it on to Jenny. Jimmy was now sitting in a small overstuffed desk chair next to her cot.

"Okay, why don't you lay down now, before you know it you'll feel very relaxed and will probably fall asleep," Jake said as he returned her smile. "Jimmy and your Dad will be right here, so don't worry about a thing."

Mick wasn't sure how much she really understood, but he was glad she accepted their plan so readily. Charlie found another generator in the other tent and already had it up and running.

He watched Jake head straight toward the back, Mick knew Jake would be booting up the computers in the hopes that he could find out if they indeed had the cure to the virus.

If they didn't, they would have to test Brooke to see if she was one of the lucky ones whom the current vaccine wouldn't kill. Jake was almost certain that Malcolm's people didn't have the time to reformulate the vaccine to make it safe for everyone, but he had to check, and that would take time.

With another glance at his daughter, he patted Jimmy on the shoulder. "I'm going outside to talk to the boys, but I'll be right back."

At Jimmy's nod he turned and headed out to find his sons. He spotted Scott right away; he was standing in the bed of the pickup, looking out toward the meadow with a pair of night vision binoculars.

"What's got your attention?" Mick asked as he leaned against the truck.

"Hi Dad, I'm watchin' Sean do his thing."

"Do his thing? What do you mean?"

Scott held out the binoculars. "Hop on in and I'll let you see for yourself."

Mick scrambled up and switching off his flashlight, took them from his son.

"You might need to adjust them a little," Scott said. "Look over to the far left; you should be able to see him."

Mick held them up and after a few minor adjustments he was able to see Sean. He was wearing night vision goggles and was bent over something, but was too far away for Mick to make out exactly what he was doing. Then he rose up and Mick saw he carried a metal rod with a giant spike coming out of the side.

Mick grunted. "Let me guess, he's out there killing zombies."

"Yep, he couldn't take it any longer, those things are dangerous and he said if he didn't do something about them and someone else got hurt or killed he wouldn't be able to live with himself. He's using his newest creation; he couldn't wait to try it out."

Mick couldn't blame him, if he didn't need to stay close to Brooke, he would be tempted to join him out there in the deadly field.

As they stood there watching, Mick asked, "What kind of monster is this guy? I can understand going to great lengths to try to keep your kids safe, but murdering hundreds of people to accomplish that goal? A sane person would never do such a thing, they'd find another way."

"I guarantee you one thing," Scott growled as he leaned on the cab and adjusted his glasses. "He will pay sooner or later, and I hope it's sooner."

"I agree, the whole situation is difficult enough without having to constantly watch our backs, always wondering where Malcolm and his hired thugs are."

Mick pointed toward Sean. "What is he doing now?"

"When he kills a few, he cuts them loose and puts them in a pile, that way he's got a clear area to work from as he moves in. We're planning on coming back here tomorrow if we can and burning the corpses."

"Oh," was all Mick could think of to say. The whole idea of putting zombies down and disposing of them would never sit well.

Scott picked up a flashlight next to his pack. "I need to do a little patrolling, do you want to stay here or come with?"

"I probably need to go check on Brooke, so I'll take a pass," Mick said as he handed the glasses to Scott, who returned them to his pack. "I'll be back later; hopefully I'll have some good new to pass along."

"I hope so, wish we could do more for Brooke, I hate this helpless feeling."

"We all have the same feeling," Mick said with a sigh as he gave his son a pat on the shoulder before hopping down. "Best thing we can do is keep her in our prayers."

Scott nodded and jumped down beside Mick. "Oh we've already been doing a lot of that. Praying that Jake has some good news on that cure, too."

Mick nodded. If there was one thing that would change everything it would be that there was now, indeed, a cure to the terrible curse they found themselves under. With a wave of his hand, he turned and using the light from inside the tent to guide him, headed back inside.

****

Fog was beginning to envelope them as they descended the mountain, but it didn't matter. They were close...so close he could almost smell them, especially since there were so many now.

He knew the area well, at one time when he had another agenda; he was an unobtrusive and covert observer. As they continued on, the fog grew ever thicker, shrouding them as they stumbled toward their goal.

Sudden movement ahead caused him to stop mid-stride, those

behind him froze in place. Nothing moved in the silent fog.
Patiently, he watched. His eyes were sharper now and it wasn't long before he spotted more movement. Slowly, he moved forward and almost as one, those behind him followed.

At one time he would have recognized the two men as part of Malcolm's team, but now all he knew was that they represented relief for a few of them. He stepped back and called to the ones directly behind him. Seven responded and he watched them silently descend on their prey.

The two men never saw or heard them coming until it was too late, and although they fought valiantly, it was in vain. While the seven satisfied their thirst, the rest continued on, led by the one who promised them that what they sought would soon be in their grasp.

Chapter 18

The fog was now so thick in the ditch that Cindy's flashlight was useless. Switching it off, she stopped and turned toward Casey and Judith.

"I can't see far in this fog, but I can see that right in front of us there's what looks like a small bridge going over the ditch. Why don't we rest there and wait a bit to see if the fog lets up some."

The bridge didn't offer any type of real protection, but having a place to get under and relax for a moment was appealing and they hurried underneath. Casey sat down on a small cement block that extended from the supports and pulled a brown paper sack from his rumpled and torn backpack. He handed each of them a sandwich wrapped in wax paper before pulling one out for himself. He then tossed them a bottle of water.

"I always carry a lunch with me, I never know where I'll be or how long I'll be gone, and I always carry extra," he said with a grin. He nodded toward them. "Eat up, we can use the energy."

"Don't have to tell me twice," Judith replied. She took a big bite of her sandwich and smiled. "Oh, this is good!" she said around a mouthful of homemade bread and chicken salad. She swallowed and took a big swig of water. "Didn't realize I was so hungry."

Everyone ate in comfortable, but watchful silence, grateful for the break. As the fog grew thicker around them, it seemed to offer a sense of protection. Slowly however, Cindy began to feel a tinge of uneasiness. She threw a furtive glance at Judith and Casey. Casey was fussing with his backpack and Judith was finishing her sandwich, neither one seemed the least bit nervous or anxious.

She tried to dismiss her feelings and set about finishing up her own sandwich. As she placed the wrapper and empty water bottle in her pack, she couldn't ignore what she felt anymore. She stood up.

"The fog is so thick, I think it's actually safer to travel now than earlier," she said in a low voice, worried that the sound would carry. "We know our way around better and should be able to stay away from any of the

Connor Group people. I've been thinking we should head for the other road first though, it's closer. Let's see what the patrol there has encountered and decide if we want to stay there or go on to the main road to try and find Dexter and the others. What do you say?"

Judith stood and stretched. "Sounds like a plan to me." She turned to Casey. "Are you ready to head out?"

Casey nodded and stood slowly, grimacing slightly as his bones creaked with movement. "Give me a minute to grease the gears and I'll be good to go," he said with a chuckle. As he hobbled up and down between the bridge supports a few times, both women shouldered their packs and checked their weapons.

There were two roads into Shady Oaks, the main road that eventually led to the highway, and a two lane blacktop into Harris. The dirt road that led up the mountain to where Mick and the others were branched off from the blacktop.

As they continued on, Cindy hoped that someone there might know something so they would know what to do next. She was nudged out of her reverie by a sharp elbow to her upper arm.

She jerked her head up to look at Judith. "What was that for?"

Judith frowned and held a finger to her lips. "I'm hearing something. Listen."

Both women stood silently, watching Casey totter on in front of them.

"Casey!" Cindy hissed. When he stopped and slowly turned, she waved to him. "Come back!"

When he reached them, Cindy placed a hand on one skinny shoulder. "Judith heard something, we need to figure out where it's coming from."

Casey nodded and they stood together silently for what seemed like several seconds. Then they all froze when they heard the sound, one they all hoped to never hear again. There was a group of zombies somewhere, of that they were certain. Nothing else produced the groaning, moaning, and wheezing noises that came and went in the fog.

Cindy pointed up to her right. "I think the road is right up there, let's see if we can find a good spot to climb up."

After quickly scanning the ditch, they were unable to find an easy route and ended up climbing at an angle. The going was difficult, the grass was covered in thick dew from the fog and they kept slipping. Both women had Casey by an arm and they grunted with the effort of pulling him along. Reaching the top, they stopped and clung to each other, trying to catch their breath.

A few minutes passed and still panting lightly, Cindy straightened and looked around. As far as she could tell, nothing moved in the fog. She stepped onto the street and pointed. She could faintly see the two large oak trees that graced either side of the entrance to the blacktop road, but was unable to tell if anyone was there.

"Look, we're not too far off, let's get going."

"Casey, are you ready?" Judith asked in a low voice. She was concerned, they were asking a lot from him.

He ran a shaky hand over his face and nodded. "I think I'll be all right if we move a little slower," he murmured apologetically. "That climb took a lot out of me."

214

Judith smiled and once again took him by the arm. "No problem, we'll take our time, the road is close. Let me help you for a bit."

"We're not sure where those zombies are," Cindy said once they reached her side. "So keep your eyes peeled."

"We need to slow the pace for a bit," Judith said as she nodded toward Casey. "Probably a good idea to approach that road slowly anyway."

"Agreed. Why don't we cross the street and hug the trees on the other side, which will give us some cover."

"Good idea."

As they walked across the street Cindy hoped that whoever was on patrol knew what was going on. She frowned when they were close enough for her to see that the barbed wire gate that stretched between the two trees was down. The gate was flimsy, but it offered the patrols some control over the road, which was important if you had to contend with dangerous problems like stray zombies or hostile people like the Connor group.

Just short of the road they stopped. Cindy shook her head.

"This doesn't feel right. Where are they?"

"I don't know, but I agree, it's too quiet," Judith said with a shudder.

"And creepy," Casey chimed in. "Maybe we should stay on the street and head on up to the main road."

Cindy was about to reply when she spotted a subtle movement from the corner of her eye. She held up a hand.

"Something's on the road."

Together they slowly moved forward until they stood between the two trees and faced the blacktop.

Cindy squinted as she scanned the road before her with the flashlight. The beam swept by a dark shape and she almost missed it. She quickly swung the light back and held it there.

"What is that?" she whispered. "I still can't make it out in this fog..."

"Look," Judith said as she pointed with flashlight in hand. "There is definitely someone standing off to the left of where your light is."

"Do you think it's the patrol? Should we chance calling out to them?" Casey asked.

"Not yet," Cindy said. She shook her head and rubbed her eyes. "I think my eyes are playing tricks on me, the longer I look the more people I think I see."

"Perhaps we should get off the road, it might be the Connor thugs," Judith murmured.

At that moment a light breeze blew around them, sending the fog tumbling and whirling. For a moment what stood before them was revealed, causing all three to gasp and automatically begin to back up.

From where they were standing, the road sloped gently down and for as far as they could see, what looked like hundreds of zombies stood on the road. They made no sound and stood still as statues.

Cindy felt as though ice was running through her veins and she could hear her heart thumping in her ears. She thought she had experienced true fear before, but knew she hadn't until now. Her mind was having problems processing what she was seeing and she reached out toward Judith, never taking her eyes off the horrors standing there staring at them.

217

Clutching her friend by the front of her jacket, she gave Judith a little shake. "Grab hold of Casey and run – head to the church and ring that bell to warn everyone. I'll go on to get help," she managed to gasp out in a weak and trembling voice. Her whole body began to shake and she took a step back. As one, the whole mass of zombies took a step forward.

Her eyes widened and adrenaline coursed through her body, replacing the ice with a fiery heat. She turned and grabbed Judith by the arm, spinning her around. Judith already had a grip on Casey. She gave them both a shove and looked back. The zombies were on the move.

"They're coming!" she cried out. "Run!" She grabbed Casey's other arm. Fueled by fear, they ran blindly down the street. Cindy couldn't think clearly and after a quick glance at Judith, she knew they were close to panicking. The first intersection they came to, she took a quick glance back and jerked to a stop.

"Okay, this is a good place for us to split up. You two go on down that way to the church," she spoke rapidly. The zombies were moving slowly, but there still wasn't much time to stand around and talk. "Be careful, but try to get there as fast as you can. I'll try to find Dexter and his group."

Judith and Casey nodded, both were panting and their eyes were large with fright.

"If you can, try to make it back to the church, we'll be waiting for you there," Judith said breathlessly. She began to move off with Casey still in tow. He gave Cindy a small smile and wave as they left.

She watched them pick up the pace before she took another quick glance behind her. "Damn," she said under her breath.

There were so many zombies they filled the street and spilled over onto both sides of the shoulder. The fog seemed to be hemorrhaging zombies, they just kept coming. Other than the sound of shuffling feet, not a sound emanated from them. She spun on her heel and ran down the road as fast as she could, the sound of her frantic breathing loud in her ears.

★★★★

When Mick returned to the tent, he went straight to Brooke's side. She seemed to be asleep and now had an IV inserted into her hand. He glanced at Jimmy who was holding her other hand.

"Jake put that in and took a blood sample," Jimmy said in a low voice. "He said the IV would deliver the vaccine right into a vein to get it into her system faster."

"Makes sense," Mick murmured. "I think I'm going to head back there and see if he's figured out anything yet." He glanced around again. "Where's Jenny and Charlie?"

"Jake sent them to the other white tent, there's some info he needs off a flash drive. Guess he found some notes on a computer telling him it might be plugged into another computer over there."

"Ah, I see," Mick said. "I'll be back in a bit."

As he turned, Jenny dashed through the entrance with Charlie right behind her. When she saw Mick she skidded to a stop in front of him and grabbed him by the hand.

"Take him over there, I'll be right there with Jake," Charlie yelled as he rushed by them and disappeared behind the plastic curtain.

Puzzled, Mick started to ask what was going on, but Jenny didn't give him a chance. "C'mon!" she squawked, jerking him by the hand.

"Okay!" he managed to say as she pulled him behind her. He stopped for a second; lunging for the flashlight he placed on a nearby desk earlier. Jenny frowned and gave him another hard jerk.

"Hurry!"

"Coming!" he shouted back at her. He switched on the flashlight as they scurried outside. He couldn't imagine what had both Jenny and Charlie acting so frantic, but he was certain that the way things were going, it wouldn't be anything good.

Emerging from the tent, he took a quick glance around. Sean was still at his gruesome task and Scott was no longer by the truck. Fog was creeping up toward the meadow from below, giving the whole area an eerie, spooky look and feeling.

Jenny gave his hand another tug and he turned to follow her. Charlie and Jake emerged and Mick was certain the puzzled expression on Jake's face mirrored his own.

Once inside the other tent, he swept the flashlight's beam

221

around. This was obviously where the real work was done on the vaccine. A divider ran down the entire length of the tent, with openings between them about every ten feet. One side housed a row of computers and lab stations, the other a row of metal exam tables with a few hospital beds partially obscured with curtains at the end. His beam faintly penetrated the darkness in the very back; he could barely make out what looked like a couple of large dog crates.

Jenny pointed her flashlight toward one of the hospital beds. "We need to go down there."

Silently they followed her down the aisle and when they reached the last hospital bed, she threw back the curtain. Mick gasped. A pale, heavily freckled young woman with fiery red hair lay there, either dead or unconscious. She looked a little older than Brooke, her left arm was covered in thick bandages and an empty IV was still inserted into her right hand.

"She's alive, we checked before coming to get you," Jenny whispered. She walked over to stand by the girl's head and brushed back a strand of her hair.

"She's been sedated, just like Brooke."

"I wasn't allowed in here," Jake said in a low voice. He moved to Jenny's side. "I bet she was just one of many that they were using as a guinea pig."

Mick walked past the bed toward the crates. He was curious. Why were they here? As he approached, he saw faint movement coming from the cage on the right. He stopped for a moment, focusing his flashlight on the spot. He stepped closer, still trying to figure out what he was looking at.

"Oh," was all he managed to say. He took a deep breath and closed his eyes for a second before peering down once more. A zombie lay in the bottom of the cage, a quick glance confirmed the other cage also held a zombie.

To make them fit, their arms and legs were removed. Both zombies were male, naked, and their heads were shaved. Since they made no vocalizations, he assumed their voice boxes were removed like the zombies in the meadow. They looked like giant bruised slugs except for their eyes, which were currently glaring at him.

"When we saw all this, we came running for you and Jake," Charlie said in his ear. Mick started, he was so engrossed with what was before him he hadn't heard Charlie come to stand beside him.

"I knew Malcolm was a dangerous man, but I had no idea the lengths he would go to save his son." He turned to his friend and held up his hands.

"My daughter is in the same situation, but I could never do something like this, it's just not in me."

Charlie patted him on the shoulder. "Yeah, don't think there are many people out there who would. How do you even think of this stuff? Staking zombies to the ground, keeping them in cages, cutting them up and removing or damaging their voice box so they can't make any vocalizations? Who does that?"

"A psychopath, that's who," Jenny interjected. She and Jake joined them and they all stared at the wriggling creatures. "The only thing Malcolm cares for is himself and his son, which I'm guessing he sees as an extension of himself."

Jake sighed and turned. "Well, we need to get busy. I'm going to check on the girl, will

224

you three see if you can find that flash drive for me? The sooner I have the information I need, the faster I can help Brooke."

"Sure thing," Jenny said as Mick and Charlie nodded. "Mick why don't you start at this end and we'll go up front, then we can meet in the middle."

"Sounds like a plan," he said distantly. His focus was still on the caged zombies. He gave himself a mental shake and hurried over to the first computer. A quick scan revealed no flash drive so he went to the next. To his surprise, there it was, sticking out of a port. He jerked it free and held it up.

"Found it!" he shouted with a wave of his flashlight. He headed for Jenny and Charlie. When he reached them, he held it out for them to see. Jenny slowly brought up her hand, she was holding a flash drive, too.

"Oh, that's great," Mick said sarcastically. Now Jake had two flash drives to look through.

"Let's show him what we've got," Jenny said as she brushed past him.

As they headed toward Jake, Mick could see him leaning over the unconscious girl. Someone found and placed a battery-operated lantern on the metal chest next to the bed, illuminating the area and chasing away shadows so he could examine her.

When Mick reached the foot of the bed, the girl's eyes opened and she began to scream. Jake jumped back in surprise. Jenny ran over to the girl's other side and took her hand.

"Shh! You're okay, we'll get you out of here," Jenny said in calm, soothing voice. After a few moments, the girl wiped away her tears and ventured a glance at the group around her bed.

"Who are you people?" she managed to gasp out between sniffles. Jenny found a box of tissue and handed her one.

"We're from Shady Oaks; some of us stumbled onto this place. A lot happened today, but don't worry about that," Jenny replied with a smile. "Now why don't we introduce ourselves and you can tell us what you're doing here."

"I'm Beth. I don't know how long I've been here; I did live over in Harris and was hiding out with my boyfriend and his parents when the Connor people took us."

Beth sat up in bed. "My boyfriend, his name is Hunter, have you seen him or his parents?"

"You're the first person we've seen that doesn't belong to the Connor Group," Charlie interjected. "We'll look for Hunter and the others as soon as we can."

"Why are you here?" Jake asked. While Beth was talking, he had slowly removed the IV and was now gently freeing her from the restraints that kept her confined to the bed. "Did you have an accident?"

Sudden fear filled her eyes. "No, I didn't have an accident! After they strapped me down some doctor, if that's what you can call him, took one of those things out of its cage and let it bite me." She shuddered and closed her eyes as another tear rolled down her cheek.

Jenny gave her hand a gentle squeeze. "We know this is hard for you, but can you tell us what they were trying to do?"

"Oh, I can tell you, they loved to brag about what they were doing. I guess the vaccine they developed doesn't work for everyone. First they drew blood; they had some new test that would tell them if a person could be cured of infection. Of course they told me this after I was bitten, but they also said it looked as though the vaccine would work for me."

Jake nodded thoughtfully. "So we know they don't have a new cure, only a new test. I figured as much, they just didn't have the time." He looked at Beth. "When did all this happen?"

Beth pursed her lips together as her brow furrowed in thought. "I was already running a high fever when they gave me the injection and then sedated me so things are kind of fuzzy, but I do remember someone saying it was almost dinner time."

"Okay, let's say you probably received the injection about three hours ago. From what I can tell by doing a quick exam, your fever is gone and you seem to be fine."

He pointed to her arm; he had finished removing the bandage. The bite on her forearm was deep and closed with butterfly stitches, but the color looked good. "Apparently the vaccine did its job."

She smiled up at him. "So I'm all right? I want to get up then, I need to find Hunter. They were keeping us in a smaller tent and I'm pretty sure I can find it again."

Jake nodded and Jenny helped her sit up and swing her legs over the edge of the bed. "Sit for a moment before getting up," Jenny urged.

Jake walked over to Mick. "We have the info on the flash drives, which we're definitely going to find useful, but at least we know where they left off without me having to waste time looking. I already have a sample of Brooke's blood, so I need to get over there and get it tested."

"So what's in those vials is what you need to test her blood?"

Jake nodded as he headed toward the entrance with Mick walking along. "I'm fairly certain that's what it is, but I won't know until I actually start testing. Once we complete the test we'll know if she will tolerate the vaccine."

Mick nodded grimly. "I hate to ask, but what will we do if the test shows she can't handle it?"

Jake paused long enough to look at Mick. "I go through the flash drives to see how far they got on the new vaccine. Then I have to try and produce enough of

229

the vaccine to inoculate her in time."

"I think what you're telling me is that we need for this vaccine to work or we could lose her."

Jake sighed and ran a hand through his already tousled hair. "I'm not going to sugar coat this. Yes, we need for it to work because I think it will take too much time to develop the new vaccine. Unless you want to put her in a coma like Connor, but let's see what happens first."

Mick winced at the thought of Brooke lying comatose, waiting for a vaccine that may never come. As they entered the tent, he pasted a smile on his face so if she were awake, she wouldn't know just how worried he was.

****

Before reaching the town, he stopped and waited until all stragglers joined them. Then, under his tight control, they began to move as one. He knew exactly where they should go and how to get there.

By coincidence, he had been to Shady Oaks many times in the past when he was still human, his wife grew up there. When Malcolm was scouting the area for a place to set up base camp, it was his suggestion that they use the lake area on the mountain.

He wanted to avoid running into anyone for as long as possible, but before even entering the town they were seen and heard. Now he urged them to move faster and they surged onto the road, quickly turning down a side street, going the same direction as Casey and Judith. He watched a lone figure running away from them, but he had no interest. He knew there would be a lot of people in the center of town and with his numbers, they would easily overwhelm and destroy them all.

Growls, groans, and moans caught his attention and with a growl of his own, he quickly brought his focus back to the others. They required constant urging to keep quiet and to continue to move forward as a group.

He projected an image of them feeding and gorging themselves as their reward for following him. The group once again grew silent as they eagerly moved forward, their collective consciousness

allowing them to move as one
entity ever closer to their goal.

Chapter 19

Cindy ran until the pain in her side made her walk. Gasping for air, she hurried along, fear making her jog after only a few steps. She had to get to the others and let them know what was coming. Between the zombies and the Connor Group, she was deeply afraid for the people in the small town that she'd come to love.

The sound of rapid gunfire made her jump and duck down. She had no idea where it was coming from, but it sounded close. She scurried across the street to the row of houses lining the road on her left. The closest house had several thick bushes a little taller than her along the front, and she quickly slipped behind them. She worked on slowing her breathing so she could listen. Straining to hear, she was certain she could hear faint shouting and she jumped again when there was more gunfire.

"Damn," she muttered under her breath. She was fairly certain what she was hearing was coming from downtown, most likely close by where Judith and Casey were. If that were the case, they would probably have to wait to warn the others, and that could be disastrous.

She stood silently for several more seconds, becoming acutely aware of how alone she was. She slowly peered out. The fog seemed to be thinning a bit, and she checked up and down the street for movement. Satisfied that all was still, she carefully slid out from between the bushes and hurried across the lawn and back out onto the street. She knew where she was and quickly picked up the pace again, jogging toward her destination.

Through the fog she could make out a faint glow, which meant the main road was up ahead. They always kept a lantern shining at night to let everyone know all was well. If the light wasn't there, it told people not to come closer, that something was wrong and to wait for someone to come and let them know when it was safe to proceed into town.

Despite the light, Cindy slowed down and once again strode over to the nearest house. There was an attached carport with a recessed entry leading to a side door, and she ducked inside the small space. From her vantage point, she could still see the light. What concerned her was other than the light, the road seemed deserted.

She scanned the area and as she was about to head out, she heard a cough. She froze for a second then stepped back into the darkness. She squinted and could barely make out two figures hurrying toward her position.

With shaking hands, she carefully reached down to unholster her gun and held it against her chest. The two figures grew still and one coughed again. When the other person shushed them, Cindy's eyes grew wide.

She stepped out. "Megan? Darrell?" she called softly. "It's me, Cindy!"

One figure stepped away and hurried over. Cindy smiled as Megan gave her a hug. "Cindy! What are you doing out here alone?"

"Am I glad to see you two, we've been trying to find you all day," she said as she returned the hug.

When Darrell joined them, she quickly brought them up to speed on the day's events.

"We wanted to get hold of you via the walkies, but we had to maintain radio silence," she explained.

"Don't blame yourself, we understand and we know Jimmy's safe for now," Megan murmured reassuringly.

"We did run into Dexter a little while ago, he only stopped long enough to let us know about the Connor mercenaries, said they somehow infiltrated the town without being seen." He paused, scratching the top of his head. "Wonder why he didn't say anything about Jimmy?" Darrell asked.

"Well, unfortunately that's Dexter for you," Cindy replied. "As for the Connor people, Judith and I had a close call with them at the hardware store, they came in the front and we went out the back."

"Dexter said Mark told him the military guys are headed this way, have you seen them?" Megan asked.

Cindy started to reply, but the sound of more gunfire stopped her. She gave her friends a sad look. "Sounds like it's getting intense. Even though we're not supposed to, I'm going to hail Mick on the walkie. We really need help and need it now."

She unclipped the walkie from her hip and after fiddling with the dial, walked back over to the carport with Megan and Darrell following. She realized no place was really safe, but at least the house offered them some cover while she talked to Mick.

"Mick, come in Mick," she said in a firm but low voice. "Please respond, this is an emergency."

She frowned and bit her bottom lip. Just as she was about to key up again, she heard a crackle then Mick's voice came across.

With a sigh of relief and flashing a quick grin at her friends, she hurriedly began to tell Mick what was happening in Shady Oaks.

****

When he first heard Cindy's voice, Mick jumped in surprise. He was standing just inside the tent, watching Brooke sleep, Jimmy still sitting next to her.

He quickly snatched up the walkie off his hip and walked outside.

"Cindy, I'm here," he answered. "What's going on, are you okay?"

"Not really," she replied. She said something else he couldn't hear due to static and he fiddled with the squelch.

"Say again, didn't hear you."

"I'm at the main road with Darrell and Megan. We have a gunfight going on in what sounds like the middle of town and at least a couple hundred zombies are headed that way."

Mick winced. So that's where they went. "Have you seen Captain Sears and his men? They should be there by now."

"You're not with them?" Cindy was puzzled. "Where are you? When Mark told us they were coming, I thought you and everyone else would be with them."

Once again, Mick knew he was going to tell a lie. There was no way he was telling her what happened to Brooke over the walkie.

"Jake wanted to come back to camp and pick up as much of the medical supplies and research as we could bring back with us - this is important stuff."

Cindy rubbed the center of her forehead with two fingers. She partially turned away from her friends and lowered her voice. "I can understand that, but Mick, I'm scared and I need you here now. Maybe Sean and Scott could bring you down here; I think we can use all the help we can get right now."

Mick closed his eyes. What was he going to do? He took a deep breath. "I would love to be there, but I don't if that's possible right now. Tell you what, let me talk to Jake and I'll get back to you in a few minutes, okay?"

"Okay, I'll be waiting," Cindy replied. He could tell from the sound of her voice that she was about to cry.

"I'll go talk to him right now," he said in what he hoped was a reassuring voice. "Stay where you are and hang in there. I love you."

"I love you too, hurry and talk to Jake," came her reply.

"Give me just a couple minutes and I'll be right back to you."

"All right."

Mick ducked back inside and immediately spotted Jake standing next to Brooke and talking to Jimmy. Jake glanced at him and Mick waved him over. He said something else to Jimmy, patted his shoulder and strolled over to Mick.

"What's up?"

He nodded toward his daughter. "How's she doing?"

"She has a low grade fever, but it doesn't seem to be bothering her. I'm running the

239

test on her blood now and it's going to take awhile to get the results, so we're going to be playing the waiting game for about three hours."

"I got a call on the walkie from Cindy; things are getting pretty bad down in Shady Oaks. Malcolm's people and the zombies both showed up. Sears and his men aren't there yet. She's begging me to bring the boys down there to help them out. I didn't have the heart to tell her what was going on and I don't know what to do."

Jake tilted his head and waved a hand toward Brooke. "I think if you want to take your boys and head down there, it would be all right. She's not going to wake up for awhile. Seems as though we're fairly safe up here because it sounds like all the bad guys are down in Shady Oaks."

"So you think it would be okay for us to run down there and help out?"

Jake nodded. "I don't expect her status to change for awhile, most likely you can go and be back before she even realizes you left."

Mick looked down at his feet for a few seconds before slowly nodding his head. For the moment, there was nothing he could do for Brooke that wasn't being done. On the other hand, his wife and friends back in town needed help now.

"I believe she's in good hands and if you say she'll be fine, then I guess we'll be heading out. I'm going to go find the boys."

"I'll let Jenny and the others know, try to keep us posted on what's going on down there if you can."

As he walked out, flicking on his flashlight to light his way, he remembered times in his life where he had grumbled to Cindy about how humdrum and tedious their daily routine was. She was always able to put things in perspective and help him see how lucky they were. How he wished for those times now, when his life was predictable and comfortable. For a moment, he felt an almost unbearable ache and sense of loss for the way of life all of them had and took for granted, and would probably never fully regain.

He passed the pickup and flicked the beam around the foggy field to find his sons. After a few sweeps, he finally picked out Scott standing at the far end of the field. He was standing next to

241

Sean, who finished dragging another zombie over to the growing pile of bodies. He waved and Mick waved back.

He cupped his hands around his mouth. "Can you and your brother come over here for a minute? Need to talk to you," he yelled across the field.

Scott nodded as Sean looked over. Sean finished tossing the zombie's body on top of the others with Scott's help and they jogged across the field, the beams of their flashlights bobbing along before them.

Mick quickly told them the details of Cindy's call and both of them nodded. "Sure, we'll take you down there," Sean said. "We need to clean up real fast, but then we should be ready to go, so get what you need and meet us at the truck."

Mick scurried back inside and after a quick glance at his sleeping daughter, grabbed his backpack and told Jake they were leaving. Once again, Jake assured him they would take good care of Brooke and when he glanced at Jenny she gave him a smile.

Charlie was still with Beth helping her search for her people. Once he got to the truck, he saw

Charlie emerge alone from the other white tent.

"Still haven't found Hunter and the others and Beth needed a break," he explained as he approached.

"Jenny told me you're leaving and I'd like to go with you, but I think it's best I stay here just in case they need me. If things go well, maybe you can bring both Cindy and Judith back with you," Charlie said as he handed Mick another backpack.

"Jenny threw some sandwiches and water in there, she's been checking out the camp and apparently found a kitchen somewhere."

"Tell her thanks," Mick said as he placed it in the bed of the truck with his other pack.

"I'm assuming you're coming back as soon as you can, Jake said you'd let us know via the walkies what's going on. Don't worry about Brooke, I promise we'll take good care of her and Jimmy, too."

"I know you will, and thanks," Mick said as they watched Sean and Scott walk over and threw more bags in back. Mick climbed into the truck bed as his sons got inside and Scott started the engine. He felt too fidgety to ride in the back seat.

"Tell Judith I'm sorry," Charlie said as he stepped back from the truck.

Scott turned the truck around and they headed slowly toward the dirt road. They would have to drive carefully around and down, but at least they were on their way.

Mick saw Charlie wave his flashlight at them, then turn and disappear inside the tent. Settling in amongst all the gear, he tried to make himself as comfortable as he could for the bumpy and dusty ride down to Shady Oaks.

The main thought that continually ran through his head was that they get there in time to make a difference. If something happened to Cindy, too, he would never be able to forgive himself. Before talking to her again on the walkie, he closed his eyes and said a silent and heartfelt prayer for all of them.

★★★★

They were moving along at a good pace until the sound of gunfire threw everything into

chaos. Zombies began to break off
from the group to follow the
sound, their minds abuzz with
anticipation. They all knew
instinctively to follow sounds; it
often paid off with a good chance
to feed.

He knew as they got closer to
the center of town that he would
lose some of them, but he wasn't
ready for that to happen yet. He
stopped for a moment and as a low
groan escaped past his rotting
lips, he focused on the others.

Once again he projected a
scene of where he wanted to go to
their collective minds. He showed
them a picture of their prey, ripe
for the taking. Then he showed
them chasing down their prey and
feasting on flesh.

When he sensed he was
regaining their attention, he went
further. He could feel his own
excitement growing as he filled
their minds with images of
ripping, tearing, biting, and
eating. Sucking the juices and
blood from fresh meat, feeling the
surge of energy and even a form of
basic pleasure, made it all
worthwhile even if it only lasted
a short time.

He was becoming more
dehydrated and wanted to pick up
the pace before he lost them all

for good. If that happened, he was certain they would be hunted down and destroyed, their sheer numbers were the only thing that gave them an advantage. The thing that drove him onward demanded that not happen and that they attain their goal.

They came to an intersection and through the thinning fog he could see that the road to his left led to the park and the buildings on the other side.

Without hesitation, he turned and led his army of the dead onward.

Chapter 21

Cindy paced back and forth across the yard with the walkie tightly clutched in one hand. She was waiting for Mick to call her back, but time was running out. Cindy glanced at Megan and stopped in front of her friend.

"Okay, so I guess I will head back down the road to see if I can intercept the captain and you two are going to head downtown, right?"

Megan nodded. "We're going to walk with you most of the way though, it's too dangerous for you to go back down there alone."

Darrell was standing in the road, waiting for them. He was ready to get going and was growing impatient. He was about to head back over to them when he heard the faint hum of an engine. He froze, listening carefully. Sure enough, he heard it again and grinned.

"Hey!" he said in a loud whisper. "I hear engines and I'm betting anything it's Sears and his men!"

Cindy tilted her head to listen, and then nodded. "I can hear it, too. Let's move back over

to the house until we know for
sure it's them."

Once more hidden under the
carport entrance, they waited
patiently as the noise of several
vehicles grew louder and it wasn't
long before they were able to see
lights. Sudden movement made them
freeze, there were several
soldiers walking silently along
either side of the road.

Without thinking, Darrell
rushed out and down the front
yard, waving his hands and
shouting. Almost immediately, he
was surrounded and knocked to the
ground. Megan shook her head and
groaned, muttering something about
men.

They could hear Darrell
talking rapidly and when several
heads turned their way, they
slowly stepped out with their
hands up in the air. Two soldiers
broke off from the group and ran
over to them, shining flashlights
in their eyes and causing them to
squint and turn away.

"We're the good guys, you can
stop that now," Megan growled as
she turned back and gave them what
Darrell called "the look."

To Cindy's surprise, they
lowered the flashlights and
stepped back. Once the light was

out of her eyes, she realized she knew one of the soldiers and gave him a smile, which he returned. "Wait here," he said as he turned to scamper down the road.

Megan and Cindy joined Darrell and the remaining soldiers on the side of the road. The first vehicle Cindy could make out was a jeep and the soldier she had just spoken with was now riding in the back, with Captain Sears sitting in the passenger seat. She was never so happy to see anyone in her life.

The three of them rushed over and began talking excitedly all at once. He chuckled and held up a hand. "Hold on!"

They stopped and when Megan gave Cindy a nod, she took a deep breath and hurriedly filled him in on what had transpired since she and Judith had to leave the hardware store. He listened intently, interrupting a few times to ask questions.

"So let me see if I have this straight. The townspeople are probably in the center of town with some patrols here and there." At her nod, he continued. "Malcolm's men are most likely surrounding them and trying to find a way to get the advantage.

Then we have the zombies and last of all, us."

Cindy nodded. "That sounds about right. Sean and Scott are bringing Mick in, too. I was beginning to panic a little and couldn't help calling him."

"I know, we picked up your transmission," he replied. At her crestfallen look, he grinned and reached over to pat her arm. "Don't worry, I'm sure the last thing Malcolm is concerned about is a couple of people coming in late to a gunfight."

"I guess you're right," Cindy replied. "So what should we do now?"

Before he could reply, the sound of church bells rang out loud and clear. At the sound, everyone stopped what they were doing and listened. In the thinning fog, the sound had an eerie quality and Cindy felt a shiver run down her spine. Almost as soon as the last note faded away, there was the sound of gunfire followed by two large blasts.

"That doesn't sound good," Captain Sears said with a frown. "I want you three to stay here and wait for Mick and your sons - we're already in the process of setting up a perimeter around town and we're going to slowly move in." He pointed a finger at Cindy and her friends. "Don't come into town until you hear from us, I don't want you getting hurt, understand?"

At their solemn nods, he gave them a curt smile and turned to his driver. As the jeep began to move off, he turned in his seat. "One of you set your walkie to Channel 3," he instructed and with a wave he turned back.

"I'll set mine," Darrell said.

"Okay," Cindy murmured as they watched the rest of the soldiers and vehicles go by. She wanted Mick there now and was beginning to feel anxious again.

As the last vehicle turned the corner at the end of road and headed toward town, Cindy heard the familiar crackle of her walkie. She snatched it up and waited.

"Cindy! Can you hear me?" Judith's voice came over loud and clear and she turned it down a bit.

"I hear you, I just talked to Captain Sears and they're headed your way."

"Well, it won't be a moment too soon," Judith replied with

what sounded like panic in her voice. "We rang the bell, did you hear it?"

"I don't think anyone could help but not hear it," Cindy said.

"Well, the people in the shelter heard it too, and they thought it meant they could come out."

Cindy heard more gunfire and the walkie was silent for several moments. She was afraid to break the silence and waited. When Judith returned, she was whispering.

"This is bad," she said in such a low voice that Cindy had to turn the volume up again.

"What's going on?"

"Almost as soon the people started coming out, most were rounded up by the Connor people, some got away. They're holding them right next to city hall."

Cindy grimaced. "So no one realized you were warning them, that's really bad."

"Tell me about it, what do we do?"

"Not sure, Darrell and Megan are with me, let me talk to them and I'll get right back to you."

"Copy that."

She hoped they had some ideas, she had nothing. As she

looked at Darrel, she noticed something over his shoulder. She knew it was a vehicle, but the lights were off and it was flying down the road. Before they could react, the truck pulled up and slid to a stop. Scott was driving with Sean in the passenger seat. To her relief, Mick popped his head over the cab of the truck and gave her a quick wave before climbing over to envelop her in a big hug.

★★★★

Charlie checked to make sure everyone was all right before heading back to help Beth resume her search. He found her digging through a white mini-fridge. She straightened up and smiled at him. "My favorite, orange soda," she said with a small grin as she gave the can a slight shake.

He grinned back and tossed her a small bag of chips. "Sorry it's not more substantial, but Jenny wants us back in about fifteen minutes, she's been making a pile of sandwiches and expects us to eat all of them."

"I'm beginning to think we're not going to find Hunter, his parents, or anyone else in the

253

tents," he said as she tore open
the bag and stuffed several chips
in her mouth. Amused, he watched
her until she chased them down
with a large gulp of soda.

"I'm thinking we should check
out that other building by the one
that held all the zombies."

Beth nodded, wiping her mouth
with the back of her hand. "Good
idea, if there's no one there, we
can work our way back."

"When you're ready we'll head
over."

"I'm ready now; I can eat
while we walk." She flicked her
flashlight beam toward the
entrance. "Lead the way."

Once outside, Charlie broke
into a jog despite the thickening
fog. He wanted to get this over
with and get back inside, no
telling what was still out there.
Reaching the building he realized
it was constructed mostly of a
simple wood frame and covered with
thick plywood, clearly meant to be
a temporary structure.

He tried to look through the
single small grimy window, and
immediately felt ridiculous
because it was dark and of course
he couldn't see a thing. After a
quick, sheepish glance at Beth, he
reached over and tried the door.

To his relief, the knob turned easily.

Without hesitation he opened the door, which fortunately swung back quietly. Stepping on the threshold, he felt around for a light switch. He knew there should be power because he could hear the hum of a generator. The switch was right next to the door and he flipped it on before entering, with Beth right on his heels. She quickly shut the door behind them. Turning off their flashlights, they stood for a moment, looking around the room.

A lot of communications equipment, two desk lamps, and several maps were scattered over folding tables lining the wall on their left. A beat up black leather couch with several rips was on the right, a folded blanket with a pillow on top at one end told Charlie someone used it as a bed. The only other things in the room were a mini-fridge and an army locker. In back was another door and it was closed.

Charlie approached the door and hesitated. He placed an ear against the door to listen. If he learned one thing in the last few months, it was to never barge into an unfamiliar place. Once again, he tried the door and this time it was locked. He groaned silently and turned to Beth.

"Locked, let's see if we can find a key."

Beth immediately turned and began rummaging through the maps. Charlie decided to check out the locker after running his hand along the top of the door and coming up empty. There was a lock, but it was open. He pulled it free and was about to open the locker when Beth let out a low whoop.

He turned to see her spinning a set of keys around on one finger. She held them out to him and after standing took them from her with a smile.

"Now to figure out which one works and to do that quietly," he whispered. After a quick examination of the keys, he picked one and tried it in the lock, turning the key slowly. He smiled to himself when the door unlocked with a short click. He placed his ear against the door and listened again. Satisfied, he turned the knob and swung the door open. He quickly reached around the jamb and flicked the light switch on.

He could sense Beth right behind him, he was certain she was trying to see past him. They both gasped at the same time and rushed into the room.

Over two thirds of the room was divided by sturdy steel bars and on the other side there seemed to be at least ten people huddled together and trying to sleep on the floor.

As soon as the light came on, several of them jerked awake and scrabbled toward the back of their cell. One young man, with long tangled black hair and deep blue eyes, jumped to his feet and stepped up to the bars. He smiled through severely cracked lips and held out a hand through the bars.

"Beth, you're all right! Am I glad to see you!"

Charlie handed Beth the keys. "You let them out, I'm going back to the other room to see if there's any food or water in that fridge."

She snatched the keys from him and scurried over to the cell door. The first key she tried didn't work, but the second did the trick. He watched an older couple, whom he assumed were Hunter's parents, join their son at the now open door before leaving the room. They were all standing now and every one of them was dirty, disheveled, and malnourished.

Charlie shook his head, feeling anger building up in him against Malcolm again. The man is a monster in the truest sense of the word, he thought to himself as he bent down and opened the door to the mini-fridge.

He smiled and quickly grabbed two six-packs of water and a package of candy bars. Straightening, he glanced around the room, and then hurried over to the locker and upon raising the lid, smiled again. Jackpot. Whoever played guard obviously liked to snack. The locker was full of chips, cookies, candy, and other items Charlie hadn't seen in months.

He could hear a lot of talking in the other room and after grabbing as much as he could carry, hurried back. Beth was handing out blankets that were neatly stacked on a small wooden table. Charlie deposited his loot next to the remaining blankets and turned to Beth.

"I need to get back to the others and see how things are going; do you have it handled here? They probably should stay here for awhile to rest and refuel, and this is probably one of the safest places to be right now."

"I'm a little tired, but so excited that we found them. We'll be fine," she said with a little wave of her hand, all her attention focused on Hunter and the others.

He gave everyone a quick glance and a smile. Some smiled back while others gave him fearful and wary looks. He couldn't blame them and with a nod he turned and headed back.

He knew it was probably too soon, but he couldn't help himself, he was eager to find out if Jake's tests were finished yet and whether Brooke could handle the vaccine. He could picture calling Mick and the rest of the family on the walkie to give them the good news.

He was so engrossed in his daydream that he bumped into someone blocking his way just inside the tent. He jerked his head up in surprise and once he realized who was standing before him, his smile faded away.

"Well, look who decided to join us," said the smooth, cultured voice. "We came in the back way and surprised Jake over there."

As Malcolm chuckled, Charlie quickly glanced around the room. Everyone was either seated or standing next to Brooke, who was still hooked up to the IV and covered up to her waist with a thin green military style blanket. Malcolm's bodyguard and the two guards from earlier stood nearby, weapons in hand.

Malcolm grabbed him by the shoulder and gave him a hard shove toward the group. Charlie jerked away and grimaced angrily. Unless they could figure something out or there was some kind of miracle, there would be no call to Mick or anyone else.

Then he remembered Beth and the others and mentally crossing his fingers, hoped they would somehow notice what was going on and stay away and out of danger. Who knew, perhaps they would even figure out a way to help. Charlie took a seat next to his daughter and turned to glare at the man he hated with every fiber of his being.

"As I was saying before I was so rudely interrupted," Malcolm said with a steely glance toward Charlie. "Imagine my surprise when we returned and found all of you here. I was sure everyone had cleared out, but no, here you are." His eyes narrowed as he walked toward them. "Now why is that?" He pointed toward Brooke. "She had an accident?"

"You could say that," Jake growled.

Charlie looked at him in surprise; Jake always spoke softly and had a gentle way about him. Now he was red in the face and stood rigidly with clenched fists.

"Those *things* you put out in the field, some of them got loose and one of them scratched her on the leg and ankle. I've started running tests to see if she can handle the vaccine when you interrupted."

Malcolm's eyes widened in surprise. "Sorry to hear that, I'm assuming you sedated her?"

Jake nodded slowly, never taking his eyes off Malcolm. "From what your people discovered before leaving, we can test first to see if she will accept or reject the vaccine. If she accepts it, we'll give it to her right away. If not, we'll put her in a coma like Connor until we figure out how to make this vaccine more accommodating, which I do believe

261

can be done with a little more time. We're very close."

Malcolm stared at Brooke while absentmindedly stroking his chin. "That's why we came back, we need to finish this and get my son out of that coma. The longer he's down the harder it will be to get him back."

Once again, Jake nodded. "I'll be honest with you," he said, suppressed anger making his voice shake. "I hate what you've done with a passion; in my book everything you've done goes against what it means to be human. I think you're a monster."

He took a deep breath and continued. "However, what your staff has accomplished will save lives in the end and we need to finish what we started. So what I want to know is, will you let me join them back there, they need my help and input."

Malcolm stared at him for a moment before smiling. "Actually, I think that is an excellent idea. I know you won't try anything with your family out here and you're correct, my people can use your help and knowledge, they've already told me that themselves."

Malcolm waved a hand toward the back of the tent. "Go on, and let them know I want a report every thirty minutes."

Jake leaned over to give Jenny a quick kiss and hug before marching toward the back without another glance toward Malcolm.

"We'll be all right," Charlie whispered with what he hoped was a reassuring tone. He gave her a small, encouraging smile.

She smiled back and patted his knee. "I know, Dad, we always manage to wiggle our way out of sticky situations," she whispered back.

Charlie rubbed the back of his neck and closed his eyes. He hoped Mick was doing better than he was at the moment. Things were looking bleak. Someway, they were going to either have to take Malcolm and his men out or get word to someone about their latest predicament. At the moment though, he was fresh out of ideas, all he could do is hope an opportunity would present itself one way or another.

****

They were almost there and good thing because he was losing control. They could smell their prey, like a thirsty animal can smell water, and the thick scent that seemed to be everywhere drove them onward.

They surged toward the heart of Shady Oaks, toward the park, and the shops, and the government buildings. Collectively, they felt a jolt of energy run through them and then all control was gone.

He actually felt relief; it had been a monumental struggle to hold them. Almost as one, a great groan erupted from decaying throats, a sound that stopped the living in their tracks.

They passed the park and came upon a large group of people standing near a brick building. Once frozen in fear, when they saw what was descending upon them, they bolted and the chase was on. He watched the others fan out and before long he heard the first cries of the living as they were attacked and literally eaten alive.

He turned his mind away, he was eager to feast himself. He reached the building and stood there for a moment. He was about to turn and follow the others when he heard a sound, actually a child's cry, emanate from inside. Rapid gunfire now accompanied the yelling and screaming outside and he decided he wanted no part of that.

Silently, he stepped through the doorway, followed by several others. Together, they wandered through the lobby and office rooms until there was another cry, clearer this time. He was sure it came from below them and within moments he had found the stairs and began his slow ascent.

When he heard voices shushing the child, he sped up. Bloody, frothy drool began to spill from his mouth, dripping onto the stairs. His entire being wanted to eat, to tear and devour. He reached the bottom and stopped for a moment to digest the sight before him.

Several people stood before the open shelter door, arguing about what they should do next. A child caught his attention, her mother had her firmly by one hand and she was tugging to get away. She cried out again and as if it were a signal, they lunged forward. Since he was in front, the shoving bodies behind gave him a boost, literally throwing him *into the group of people standing there. Finally, he thought as he grabbed the first of many. Time to eat.*

Chapter 22

Mick held Cindy, several thoughts and emotions pouring through him in waves. He was still struggling with his decision to leave Brooke, hating what his grim new reality forced him to do. He didn't know what to say or do first, so he simply held her until she stepped back and smiled.

"Mom," Scott said with a wave of his hand to get her attention. "What's going on?"

Darrell and Megan joined them and Cindy once again recounted the events since Mick and her sons left Shady Oaks. As she finished, heavy gunfire drew their attention.

"Sounds like the activity is picking up, the zombies must be there," Megan remarked. "Anyone have any ideas on what would be the best way to get downtown without getting nailed by zombies or the Connor people?"

"Let's all get in the truck and head for the park," Mick said. He had been devising a plan all the way back and he hoped it was a good one. "I think from the park we can see and hear almost everything that's going on, and then decide from there what to do."

Megan headed for the back of the truck. "Sounds like a good idea, let's get going before it's over," she said as she jumped into the truck bed.

Everyone scurried to get on the truck; Mick was last and practically fell into Cindy's lap when Scott gunned it. He sat up and put his arm around his wife.

She looked up at him. "Brooke okay? I know you had to leave her up there for her own protection, but I still have this wish for us to be all together."

"She's in good hands," he said softly. How he hated not being able to tell Cindy what was really going on! "Where are Denise, Sarah, and the girls?" Mick asked. He nervously changed the subject, but also knew Scott and Sean would ask and he wanted to be ready with a reply to reassure them.

"Oh, you know how Sarah is claustrophobic so no shelter for them, she took the girls earlier today up to one of the farms, I don't remember which one. Denise is with them and they're planning on staying there tonight."

"I'm assuming the boys know where they are."

"Oh yeah, guess they planned this out just in case something happened."

"Good, that should keep them from worrying. You know they're listening, right?" Mick asked, referring to the Connor Group.

"We know, but we decided they already know we're here and it was more important we know what's going on than floundering around. Lesser of two evils stuff."

Mick nodded then winced as they hit a pothole, which bounced them all around. Just as he got somewhat comfortable, Scott hit the brakes, throwing them forward.

He stuck his head out the window. "Sorry 'bout that, think we have company up ahead."

Mick slowly stood up and climbed down, meeting Sean and Scott in the middle of the road. He flicked on his flashlight and shining it down the road, strained to see through the fog, which rolled by them in slow moving waves.

"I caught a glimpse of something in my headlights," Scott explained. "I think it was zombies and we don't want them coming this way if we can help it."

Mick placed a hand on his son's shoulder. "Glad you spotted

them, guess we should walk the rest of the way to the park."

"That's what I'm thinking, Sean and I will take lead, everyone else hang back but keep us in sight until we get there." Scott looked up at the others gathered around. "Let's hug the side of the road, no use walking down the middle and making ourselves easy targets."

He turned and after a few words with his brother, they both turned and started a slow jog with the others following at a safe distance. Watching the backs of his sons, Mick grew increasingly concerned with the gunfire and other noises they were hearing. That old feeling of being deeply scared returned and he swallowed hard, as though that would force it back down.

To his relief, it wasn't long before he spotted the beautifully carved wooden sign declaring they were at Shady Oaks Park. The entire sign looked like a giant oak tree and the words were nestled under the boughs.

Sean and Scott veered off to the right past the sign and headed down toward the small lake in the center. The lake was fed by one large creek that ran down the mountain and when spring rains came, the overflow ran down another, smaller creek that meandered out of town. Most of the farmers tapped the mountain creek for irrigation. Mick couldn't recall what the creeks were called, but decided if he survived the night, he'd do more investigating into Shady Oak's history.

Realizing he was daydreaming at the worst time ever, he shook his head and glanced up at his sons. They stopped next to the small concessions building where families often went to grab a snow cone or something cold to drink on a summer evening. Picnic tables sat under several tall oaks to provide shade from the summer heat and without a word, everyone took a seat.

Scott leaned against one table while Sean hopped up and sat on top. "Let's check our weapons while we take a quick break," he said in a loud whisper.

"Good idea," came another whisper in reply.

Mick was in the process of retrieving his gun and at first what he heard didn't register. Then he froze and looked up. Both Sean and Scott had their hands up and were looking at something behind him. He felt a hand come down on his shoulder and give a firm squeeze.

Slowly he looked at the hand gloved in black, then let his gaze travel up the arm. He took in the insignia on the uniform and then looked up at the man grimly smiling down at him. He winced. He recognized him as one of the men that had caught them up on the mountain. Casting a quick glance around, he saw they were completely surrounded, and none of them heard a sound.

"Surprise," said the man, again in a whisper loud enough for them all to hear.

Mick looked on with surprise when the man let go of him and squatted down in front of them, flanked by his army of hired help.

"Let's talk," he said in a low voice. "Who's in charge here?"

Mick felt all eyes from his group flick in his direction and he sighed. Here we go again, he thought fearfully. He straightened up and tried to look competent. "You want to talk? Well we're listening and you'd better hurry because I don't think we have a lot of time to be messing around."

"Oh, I think you'll want to hear what we propose, we can all benefit in the end."

Mick licked his lips nervously. He had an idea what they wanted. He cast a doleful eye at Cindy and she shrugged. Sighing again, he turned back.

"Talk."

****

Charlie fidgeted, his mind humming as he tried to think of some way to get out of the mess they were in. He desperately wanted to warn Beth and the others, he kept picturing over and over in his mind them walking right into the tent and back into the devious arms of Malcolm.

He leaned over toward Jenny. "How is Brooke doing, did Jake say anything when I was gone?"

"She's been sleeping through the whole thing; whatever Jake gave her is pretty powerful. The only thing he said is that the test is running, but it will be almost morning before we know for sure."

"Okay," he said morosely. He leaned back and eyed the two men still guarding them. They were the same ones from earlier in the day.

Charlie was surprised to see them; they must have been able to make their escape from Captain Sears' men during the earlier chaos.

The younger one was stationed at the tent entrance and the other man he nicknamed Bullfrog was wandering around, boredom evident on his ugly face. Malcolm and his personal bodyguard were somewhere in back.

He shifted in his chair and movement near the entrance caught his eye. He turned his head slowly, not looking directly at the opening; he didn't want to alert their guards. Slowly, a face appeared and his breath stopped as his eyes widened. Beth was looking at him and as her eyes darted downward, he finally took a breath. She saw the man in front of her and slowly drew back.

Without moving, he glanced over toward the other guard, now he was messing around with a computer. Beth reappeared and mouthed "how many" at him.

Charlie stared at the first guard and nodded slowly, mouthing "one." Then slowly turned his head to look at the other then mouthed "two" back at her. She nodded and as she went to back away he cleared his throat.

She froze and looked at him. He tilted his head and mouthed "five" as he slowly reached up as though to scratch his head. Instead he held his fingers out then pointed toward the back. To his relief, she nodded before disappearing.

He sat back and glanced at Jenny, who was looking at him with wide eyes. "I totally forgot about Beth and you didn't have a chance to tell me if you found the others," she whispered guiltily. "Do you think she can get help?"

"We found the others, they're in bad shape, but I think they can help," he whispered back. He nodded toward Jimmy, who had drifted back off to sleep himself and was currently drooling on his shirt.

"I know Jake gave him some pain medication that made him groggy, but we will probably need to wake him up soon so he can help when the time comes. If anything, he can watch over Brooke and keep her safe."

Before he could say anything more, Malcolm walked in and came to stand directly before Jenny. "My men are hungry and Jake tells me you're the person to see. I would appreciate it if you would make enough sandwiches to feed everyone. Check the fridge, there should be some fresh lettuce and tomatoes. Chips and other snack foods are in the pantry, but you probably already know what's over there."

Without a word, she stood and walked toward the back, with Malcolm following. There was a tiny kitchen area next to the lab and Charlie knew she'd be busy for awhile, so he took her seat. Now he had a better view of the entrance and wouldn't be so conspicuous if Beth returned.

He hoped Mick and everyone back at Shady Oaks were doing better; Mick would flip if he knew Malcolm was back. Charlie hated waiting and to keep from fidgeting, he slid his chair closer to Brooke and placed a hand on her forehead. She still felt warm, but not hot, and he withdrew his hand.

He glanced at Jimmy, who was on the other side of Brooke's cot. He was still asleep with one arm now outstretched on the table next to him which he used as a pillow. He didn't know how Jimmy could sleep like that, but chalked it up to being young.

The younger guard, whom Charlie decided should be called

Freckles, stood up and stretched. "I need to take a quick break," he told Bullfrog, who was still at the computers. "Be right back."

"Yeah," Bullfrog grunted with a wave, not even looking up.

Freckles shouldered his weapon and walked outside; Charlie figured he was headed for the latrines. He turned his attention back to Bullfrog.

As though he could feel he was being watched, he glanced up. "Don't try anything stupid, like before," he growled, pointing a finger at Charlie. "You won't get off so easy next time."

Charlie gave him a wide-eyed, innocent look and held out his hands, palms up. "I wouldn't think of it."

Bullfrog's eyes narrowed. "Don't play cutesy with me."

Charlie started to reply, but a strange sound from outside stopped him. Bullfrog heard it, too.

"What the...," Bullfrog said as he headed for the entrance. He almost forgot Charlie and halted. After a quick glance at Brooke and Jimmy, he strode over and grabbed Charlie by the arm. "Grab your flashlight and come with me."

Charlie went obligingly, he was certain that half cry, half choking sound came from Freckles and he was eager for Beth and the others to take care of Bullfrog, too.

He grinned to himself and had the strongest urge to start whistling, but stopped himself from acting too jubilant. Bullfrog was already on alert, a large revolver in the other hand.

"I think your friend must have run into one of those crawling zombies things that got loose," Charlie said amicably in an effort to lessen the other man's anxiety. "We'll probably run into him stomping it into the ground."

Bullfrog gave a low chuckle and to Charlie's relief, his grip relaxed a little. "Yeah, I can see that."

As they stepped outside and turned right, toward the direction of the latrines, Bullfrog pointed. "Shine your light down there."

Charlie obliged. "Looks clear to me, should we go on?"

Bullfrog just grunted and gave Charlie a shove, which he took as an affirmative and so he continued on. He hoped that what they heard was indeed Beth and the others and not some random zombies running loose, he didn't want to deal with that scenario on top of everything else.

He swung the beam from his flashlight back and forth and as they passed the second tent, he heard a noise behind them. Before he could turn around something hit him hard from behind, sending him sprawling to the ground. He gasped in surprise then grunted loudly when someone put a knee in his back. He turned his head and saw he was almost face to face on the ground with Bullfrog.

"Don't move!" Someone hissed and he froze, but then began to squirm a bit as he was gagged and his hands tied behind his back. Bullfrog was suffering the same treatment, but putting up more of a fight and from what Charlie could see in the darkness, it was taking three people to subdue him.

They were roughly yanked to their feet and hustled between the tents until they reached the end and then they took a sharp right. Charlie's arms were starting to ache as he was propelled forward; he couldn't see who had hold of him because they had a firm grip from behind on his left shoulder. He was thoroughly confused; Beth and the others wouldn't do this, so who had them?

When they reached the command center, they stopped, Charlie and Bullfrog were spun around and the same voice told them to sit against the building.

They both slid down the wall and sat on their haunches; Charlie looked away as light was shone directly in their eyes, totally obscuring their captors. He felt someone kneel next to him and stiffened.

"Charlie, it's Beth," she whispered in his ear as she patted his shoulder. "Come with me."

Grasping him by the arm, she helped him stand and led him around the building. Once inside, she hurriedly closed the door and freed him. As he rubbed the life back into his numb arms and hands, she surveyed him.

"So sorry about that, in the dark they couldn't be sure and decided it was safer that way. They're going to put the other guy with his buddy next door where the zombies were held."

"I understand, thanks for getting me out," he said with a nod. He grabbed a bottle of water from the fridge and sat down. "We need to figure out how to get everyone else out of there safely."

Beth grabbed a metal chair and sat across from him. "We talked about that and came to the conclusion that there is no way to do that without someone getting hurt, especially since two of them are incapacitated."

"True, did you come up with any ideas at all?"

Beth frowned as she looked at him, concern in her eyes. "Well, yes we did, but you're not going to like it one bit."

Charlie sighed heavily. "Tell me."

"You're going to have to go back in there and kill Malcolm."

★★★★

They feasted, although most of their prey managed to escape, some sealing themselves inside the shelter including the woman and her crying child. Some tried to fight, but they were easily overwhelmed.

With his head buried in his victim's abdomen, he shared red images of bliss with the others, stimulating the feeding frenzy. He didn't care if some escaped, for the moment there was plenty. He became satiated before the others and slowly raised his head to look around. Gore and blood dripped from his face and chest, a pool of blood surrounded him as he knelt before what was left of his feast.

The scene before him was horrific, although to him it meant success. Bodies were strewn around as zombies fed upon them, bloody entrails and body parts covered the floor, and more blood dripped down the walls. As he continued to look around, he became uneasy. He didn't like staying too long at a kill site; he preferred to pick his own place to feed at his leisure.

He stands and turns slightly, then bends down to grab the ankle of his latest victim. Dragging his trophy behind him, he slowly heads for the stairs.

With a little luck, he should be able to find a place to feed without interruption. As he passes the others, they too stand and follow him, dragging what's left of the dismembered bodies behind them.

Chapter 23

"The name is Jim Nelson, but everyone just calls me Nelson. I'm a former Navy Seal as are most of my team," the man in black said with a wave of his hand to include the men standing around him. "We were hired by the Connor Group or Malcolm directly, to provide security and to obtain whatever he asked for."

"Including healthy men, women, and children?" Mick asked. He couldn't help himself, he was certain teaming up was a bad idea with these men, regardless of the threat they faced. He was afraid after they contained the zombies, they would turn on the people of Shady Oaks.

"When Malcolm asked us to bring in people, he told us it was to insure their safety - he lied to us," Nelson said as he stood and began pacing back and forth. "Trust me, we didn't like it, but he threatened us. When we signed up, he promised to protect our families; they are all up at his compound and safe. Any time we balked or tried to reason with him, he threatened to turn our families out into the streets. He gave the same message to any

283

doctor or scientist who resisted, too."

Mick shook his head and looked away. "This decision is not up to me, we need to get hold of Captain Sears, and fast – people are dying out there right now."

Sean stepped forward. "Dad, Scott and I have a pretty good idea of where he's setting up so we're going to run over there. We'll let you know what he says, so keep your walkie close by."

Mick patted the walkie fastened to his belt. "Never go anywhere without it."

He watched his sons shoulder their packs and rifles again and as they turned to go, they heard the familiar sound of zombies nearby, followed by gunfire.

Scott pointed and everyone strained to look through the fog. "Sounds like the fight is coming to us."

"Instead of trying to find the captain, try him on the walkie," Mick said as he stood. "We've run out of time for talking. We have to act, and now!"

"Agreed," Nelson murmured as he turned to his men. "Fan out here, but stay within sight of each other. Hold your fire until they're on the street, remember to use short controlled bursts and be careful, there are civilians out there."

Sean and Scott both retreated back toward the tree line and Mick could see Sean talking on his walkie. Guess there's no more radio silence for anyone; he thought as he decided now was a good time to join them. He tapped Cindy on the shoulder.

"Grab Megan and Darrell; let's get over by the boys so we can find out what Captain Sears says."

She nodded. "All right, then we need to see if we can raise Dexter and the others."

Mick shook his head as he hurried over to his sons. Everything was becoming complicated, some kind of plan needed to come together quickly if they were going to save anyone in Shady Oaks.

Sean handed Scott the walkie as Mick approached. "Dad, they said to wait here; they're close and headed our way. I'm going to let Nelson know."

Without waiting for a reply, Sean trotted off. Scott was still talking to someone and when Mick turned to see where Cindy was, he saw her walking toward him with Darrell and Megan in tow. Darrell had his walkie out and was talking as they walked.

"I take it you were able to reach Dexter," he remarked when they reached his side.

Darrell frowned. "Yeah, but it's not good. They're all trapped at the apartments and Dexter wants to blow the stairs because he thinks the zombies will get in soon. They moved everyone upstairs and most of them are now sitting on the roof. They did have the foresight to pull the ladders up with them so they can get down, but I'm sure they won't want to stay up there very long."

Mick absentmindedly rubbed the scar on his cheek. "What a mess," he murmured. "Anything else?"

"From the sound of it, they were already on the roof when the bell rang and they saw people coming outside to see what was going on." He cast a baleful glance at Mick. "Dexter estimates maybe half got away, but the rest were swarmed by zombies."

Mick shuddered. Out of the corner of his eye, he saw the faint shine of headlights. He pointed down the road. "That must be the captain."

Everyone headed for the road and Sears jumped from his jeep before it came to a complete stop. The sounds of gunfire filled the air again as he moved toward them. Nelson and a few of his men hurried over.

Sean conducted quick introductions and while Sears reluctantly shook Nelson's hand, Scott did the talking.

"Let's cut to the chase," Sears began. He walked over to the picnic table and one of his men spread out a map and set a lantern on top. "Where are your men located?"

"We're in positions inside the town," Nelson said. "I have my men staying out of sight and out of the way right now." He pointed to several locations. "This is where we are right now. We did encounter some resistance until the zombies showed up, and then we retreated."

"All right, we've set up a perimeter that surrounds the main part of town and we haven't seen any of your men yet. Tell them to stay put and I'll insert my men to join up with yours. I'll have more men move in behind the first group to provide support and reinforcement."

Nelson nodded. "That will work; I'll get with my guys right away."

"Good idea, we'll get moving as well."

There was a sudden flurry of activity and scurrying around as everyone received their orders. Mick felt a tap on his shoulder. Cindy smiled at him and took him by the arm to walk him away from the others.

"After talking to Dexter, I got Judith on the walkie and she wanted to know if we could come help them get out of the church safely. She said there's no zombies around them right now, but that could change. Right now they're up on the second floor keeping watch and she said she'd let us know if they see anything."

"Well, I don't know how safe it is to get over there, let me talk to Sean and Scott and get their opinion," Mick replied.

"I'll ask Megan and Darrell if they want to go with us," Cindy said as Mick turned away to find their sons.

Within a few minutes they met back up, Mick with Sean and Scott, Cindy with Megan and Darrell in tow. The church was right outside the central part of town and only a few blocks away, Mick hoped they would be able to get Judith and Casey out with no problems.

"I told Captain Sears what we were planning and he said they would pass that info on so no one would mistake us for zombies, which would be easy to do in this fog. He also said there's no one by the church, so we're basically on our own once we go over there," Scott informed them.

"Then we'd better proceed with extreme caution," Mick remarked. He rubbed the scar on his cheek again as they watched the soldiers and Nelson's men head out. Slowly, they disappeared into the fog. All was silent for a moment, then the gunfire resumed, accompanied by more shouting.

Mick took a deep breath to steady himself. He looked at the others. "Guess we'd better head out ourselves," he said shakily. He took another breath and let it out slowly.

"Want Sean and me to take point again?" Scott asked as he hefted his pack up.

Mick nodded. "I think that's a good idea, but we should probably stay fairly close to you this time, the fog looks thicker over there."

"Agreed," Scott said with a nod. "Everyone should probably stay closer together, would be easy to get picked off."

They cautiously crossed the street, stopping for a moment when more shots were heard. Mick hoped they were winning the fight against the zombies, after all the work they did to rid Shady Oaks of them, it was disheartening to see the town overrun again. He could only hope most of the townspeople were able to get out of harm's way.

★★★★

Charlie ran into the tent and sat back down. He forced himself to calm down and slowed his breathing. Both Jimmy and Brooke were still asleep, he decided he would act like he was dozing too if Malcolm came back in. He could play dumb as to where the guards were. He wasn't sure Malcolm would buy it, but it would explain why they were still here unguarded and was the only thing he could think of at the time.

He slipped a hand into the right pocket of his jeans and felt the cold handle of the knife Hunter gave him. He didn't have any problems dispatching a zombie, but a human, no matter how corrupt, was a different matter. He decided to use the knife to subdue Malcolm only if he had to.

He began to relax and leaned back in the chair to get more comfortable. Jimmy mumbled something in his sleep and as he turned his head toward the boy, movement near the plastic caught his eye. Sure enough, he could see shadows moving and heard someone talking. He quickly tilted his head back and shut his eyes, allowing his mouth to fall open slightly. He hoped he looked convincing.

Chancing a quick look through slitted eyes, he saw Jenny enter first, followed closely behind by Malcolm. Quickly taking in the situation, Malcolm shoved Jenny away from him and ordered her to go sit down. Charlie continued to watch as Malcolm reached inside his jacket and he caught a glimpse of a shoulder holster. Malcolm pulled out a .45 pistol and held it up. When Jenny passed by him to sit down next to Brooke, Charlie closed his eyes and forced himself to stay still.

He heard Malcolm approach and almost fell out of his chair with surprise when he felt a hard slap to the face. He yelped and put a hand up to his cheek, looking up at Malcolm with contrived fear in his eyes.

"What did you do that for?" Charlie asked as he gingerly rubbed the reddened area. "That hurt."

Malcolm turned, waving the pistol around. "Where are they?"

Charlie sat up and rubbed his face. "Where are who?" he asked.

Malcolm turned to sneer at him. "My men, you idiot."

Charlie feigned surprise and glanced at Jenny, who was giving him a cynical look. "Um, I don't know. Guess I dozed off."

Malcolm snorted and turned again. Seeing his chance, he jumped up and wrapped one arm around the other man's neck while wrenching the knife free from his pocket. He could feel the muscles in Malcolm's back tense and he knew he was in trouble. This guy works out, Charlie thought to himself before Malcolm elbowed him in the side, causing him to grunt loudly as the breath whooshed out of him. He felt fingers over his and from the corner of his eye saw Jenny next to him. He relinquished the knife to her so he could wrap both arms around Malcolm.

Without another thought, he threw himself back, slamming into the chair he had been sitting in, with Malcolm on top. Jenny hit the thumb stud to open the knife and dropped down beside Malcolm.

"Don't move," she hissed as she pressed the wicked looking, partially serrated blade against his throat. "I would take great joy in using this."

For a moment everyone froze, and then Charlie felt Malcolm relax. He heaved a mental sigh of relief. This wasn't exactly how he pictured getting Malcolm, but the outcome could have been a lot worse.

"Jenny, let him get off me," he gasped. The man was definitely heavier than he looked.

Jenny turned the blade so the tip dug slightly into Malcolm's throat. "Sit up slowly and stay on the floor."

He complied with Charlie pushing him from behind. Soon as he was sitting up, Charlie scooted over to the side and away. He stood up and looked around for something to bind Malcolm with. He noticed Brooke was still sleeping soundly, but Jimmy was looking at him through sleep-blurred eyes.

"What's happening?"

"I'll explain later," Charlie said briskly. He pointed to an extension cord coiled neatly on the desk where Jimmy sat. "Throw me that cord?"

"Sure."

Charlie caught the cord mid-air and gave it a shake. He walked over to Malcolm. "Hands behind your back." He wanted to hurry, he knew Malcolm's personal bodyguard was in back with Jake and the others and it wouldn't be long before he came to check on Malcolm. Once his hands were tied, Charlie ran the cord down to his ankles then nodded to Jenny.

"You can back off; see if you can find something to gag him with. Try to hurry before his bodyguard comes in."

Jenny stood up and carefully closed the knife, slipping it into her pocket before looking for something to use as a gag. She stopped, thinking for a moment before hurrying over to Jake's backpack and pulling out a roll of duct tape. She then grabbed her own bag and grabbed a pair of socks. She pulled them apart and brought one over after rolling it up.

"Open up," she ordered.

Malcolm glared at her. "You won't get away with this," he spat at her angrily, his eyes shiny with malice. "You forget I have a lot more men at my disposal and they'll be back as soon as they subdue your friends down in Shady Oaks. If you don't stop this right now, there will be hell to pay."

"Oh, you're right about that," Jenny said with a deceptively sweet smile. Without warning she reared back and slapped Malcolm so hard he would have fallen over if Charlie didn't hold him up. His eyes teared up and a bright red imprint of Jenny's hand instantly appeared on his cheek.

"That's for my dad," she hissed again as she leaned forward and shoved the sock into his mouth. "Make no mistake, there will be hell to pay, but you will be making that payment – and in full."

"I'm going to see if Beth and the others are close by," Charlie said softly as Jenny slapped a piece of tape over Malcolm's gag. "They took care of the other two guys for us earlier."

She stood up, tucking a strand of hair behind one ear. She pulled out the knife and opened it again, shaking it like a finger in

Malcolm's direction. "All right, but hurry, we still have to deal with his bodyguard."

"I think I know how to handle him," Charlie remarked. "Don't worry; I'm not going anywhere, just looking outside."

The moment he stepped outside, Hunter appeared with Beth beside him. "Did you do it," Beth whispered.

Charlie shook his head. "No, we were able to take him down without killing him. He's tied up and my daughter's watching him right now."

They both looked disappointed and Charlie couldn't blame them. The man was evil and deserved to die, but not by his hand, and thankfully not by his daughter's, either.

"We still have his bodyguard to deal with; I don't think the doctors or scientists back there are any threat at all. I have a plan and I wanted to know if you can wait out here. If I yell for you, you'll know things aren't going right and I'll need for you to come and help us."

Hunter nodded. "We can do that."

"Thanks, wish me luck."

"Good luck," Beth whispered as he took a deep breath and headed back inside to put his plan into effect.

★★★★

With five other zombies, he managed to make it unmolested to his destination. Once inside, they began to feed on the dirt covered remains they brought with them. They would feed until dawn, then take what was left of their feast and retreat further down into the basement where it was dark and cool.

At this point he didn't know or care where the others were. He found it was much easier to control the ones who made the decision on some level to follow him without any type of persuasion. With their support, he was certain they would continue to be successful. Perhaps there were more who would join them, only time would tell.

He felt fairly safe where they were, the abandoned mill was a place that was out of the patrol zone and no one should bother them. He would have plenty of time to plan their next move, which would be driven by their need to feed.

Slowly, they were continuing to become more aware of the world around them, which didn't bode well for the people trying to survive. Only time would tell who would get the upper hand that could spell the difference between victory or defeat. Satisfied, he tore off another chunk of flesh from the arm he held and closed his eyes as he chewed.

Chapter 24

When they stopped so Sean could take a call on his walkie, Mick deliberately hung back. He wanted to call Charlie to see how Brooke was doing. Despite what was going on around him, he couldn't get her out of his mind. He was so worried about her and wanted to tell Cindy, but he knew it would be a really bad idea and even worse timing if he told her now. He was standing next to Scott and he tapped him on the shoulder.

"Hey," he whispered in his son's ear. "I need you to distract your Mom for a few minutes, I want to call Charlie and check on Brooke."

Silently, Scott gave him a curt nod and moved off toward Cindy. Mick turned his back to the group and holding his flashlight with one hand, quickly fiddled with the dial. His hands were shaking and it took him a moment to find the frequency.

"Charlie, come in," he said in a harsh whisper. "Can you hear me?"

"Mick! That you? What's up?" replied his friend.

"I can't talk long, but I wanted to check on Brooke. How is she?"

"She's good, still sleeping," Charlie replied. "We had a little set back here, Malcolm showed up."

Mick's blood froze and his mouth went dry. He swallowed hard. "What! Is everyone all right? I'm guessing it is or you wouldn't be talking to me."

"Everyone is fine. I can't talk for long; we dealt with Malcolm and his guards, now we're planning to take out his personal bodyguard. Beth and the others are helping."

Mick turned to check on Cindy, who was still talking to Scott, but she now had her eye on him. He turned back around. "I have to go, too," he replied. "Please take care of my little girl, Charlie."

"You got it. Jenny and Jimmy are with her now, she's in good hands."

"I know," Mick said nervously. "I will get back to you as soon as I can. Good luck on getting the other guy."

"Thanks, I don't think he'll be a problem when he sees his boss trussed up."

Despite his worry, Mick chuckled. "You're probably right. Talk to you soon."

"Copy that."

He placed the walkie back on his belt and walked over to his wife and son. He was saved from answering any questions by Scott, who was finished with his own conversation.

"They're making some progress downtown," Scott told the group. "He also said there's no one in this area so we can proceed without worrying about someone accidentally shooting us. They will rendezvous with us at the apartments to get those zombies taken care of; I'm supposed to let them know when we get there. We don't have time to waste, so let's move on out and we're not going to stop again until we get to the church."

Mick hoped once they were at the apartments that they would be able to quickly deal with the zombies there, then head across the street to join in the bigger fight. The sound of gunfire was almost constant and occasionally he could see flashes of light.

They stopped for a moment when they reached the street the church was on so Cindy could let

Judith know they were there. The church, a quaint two story building painted the traditional bright white, sat across the street on a well-manicured corner lot surrounded by large oak trees.

Judith was still watching from the second story windows and she reported no one around, so they quickly darted across. As they approached the door, they heard the dead bolt click and the door swung open. Casey stuck his head out, grinning and waving them inside.

Once he was inside, Mick looked up to see Judith hurrying down the stairs. Cindy rushed over to give her a hug.

"Good to see you too!" Judith said with a laugh as she hugged Cindy back and patted her on the back. "We're ready to get out of here!"

"Good thing because we do need to get going," Sean said with a small smile. "They're having some problems with zombies over at the apartments. No one can get in or out right now, which is hampering our ability to fight because we need every man we've got."

"I did check in that direction," Judith said as she grabbed her backpack. "The fog is

starting to lift a little and it
looked clear as far as I could
see."

Scott opened the door and
after a quick look, stepped
outside and everyone began to file
out. Mick grabbed Casey's bag when
Cindy pointed it out to him and
flipped his flashlight back on.

Sean and Scott once again
took the lead and moved cautiously
as they walked across the lawn
down to the street, turning right
and heading in the general
direction of the apartment
building. They planned to stay
about a block away until they
could slowly move in with Captain
Sears' men from the back side.
They knew there were too many
zombies on the other side that
faced and was only a block away
from the downtown area.

As they walked, Mick put an
arm around Cindy and as she
slipped an arm around his waist,
gave her a hug. He felt so guilty
and he was worried about
everything. He worried about
Brooke, even though she was in
good hands. He worried about Cindy
and his sons, he didn't want
anything to happen to them either,
and they were in extreme danger.
He worried about his friends. He
even worried about their new

homes. He hoped all their hard work hadn't been destroyed by rampaging pieces of rotting flesh.

As though she could read his thoughts, Cindy hugged him back, looking up at him and smiling. "Don't worry, you know we've been through tough situations before and we'll handle this one like we did the others – together."

Mick made a wry face and gave her another hug. "You're right, I know I need to stay optimistic, but you know me – Mr. Doom and Gloom."

She gave him another squeeze around the middle and they walked together silently until Scott and Sean came to a stop in front of them. Mick looked around; they were now at the funeral home and a short distance away from the apartments. The sound of vicious fighting was much closer now. The almost incessant shooting, coupled with a lot of shouting, yelling, and screaming was unnerving.

"We wait here," Sean said curtly. "Let's put our gear down under the overhang and rest a bit until the others arrive."

Mick sat down against the building with Cindy and the others and watched his sons as they talked together. They loved to joke around and were always the life of any party, but when it was time to get serious it was as though they flipped a switch and all joking disappeared. Mick was proud of the men they had become and how others in their new community looked to them for help and support.

Movement at the end of the street caught his attention and he saw Sean and Scott stiffen as they noticed, too. They relaxed when a few seconds later two rows of soldiers in formation came into view. They were jogging or double marching, and Mick was amazed at how quiet they were.

He heard someone give the command to halt in a low voice, but loud enough for all to hear and the soldiers stopped, still at attention. From behind, Sears' jeep swung around and pulled up to where the twins stood.

Mick and the others quickly stood up and gathered around. He didn't like the grim expression on the captain's face.

"We're going to wait a little longer, most of Nelson's men will be joining us and we're going to need them," Sears said. "Some of my men positioned at the school report downtown is completely overrun." He glanced up. "I need to get up on that roof."

"We'll make that happen," Scott replied. With a glance at his brother, who nodded, they scurried off to find a way in without drawing unwanted attention or making too much noise.

Mick turned to see Cindy talking on her walkie again. She held it out and frowning, gave it a shake. Mick knew what that meant, her batteries were dying.

Batteries were precious and all of them were tested before being deemed unusable. Sometimes only one battery was drained. He heard someone was experimenting with recharging regular batteries with limited success. He walked over and handed her his walkie.

"Thanks," she said with a grateful smile. "I was telling Dexter where we are and that we were waiting, which didn't make him too happy."

"I can imagine," Mick said as he took Cindy's walkie and flipping it over, extracted the batteries and put them in a jacket pocket. "There are not too many things that ever make that man happy."

He always tried to carry spares and as he put fresh

batteries in Cindy's walkie, Sean and Scott appeared from around the side of the building. They were running and Mick knew that whatever the reason, it most likely didn't bode well for them.

★ ★ ★ ★

Charlie put the walkie back and hurried inside to find Jenny still standing guard over Malcolm, who was shooting daggers at her with his eyes. He gave Charlie an equally fierce glare as he approached.

"So what do we do now?" Jenny asked as she gave Malcolm a nudge with her foot.

"I don't think those doctors and scientists back there are any threat, so we probably need to figure out a way to get that bodyguard up here. If Jake comes to check on Brooke, he'll be with the bodyguard and then we would have a problem."

Jenny snapped her fingers and gave Charlie a big grin. "I know what to do! I'll go back there and tell Samuel; I think that's his name, that Malcolm wants him to come up by himself, that I'm to stay and see if the rest of them need anything."

307

Charlie thought for a moment then nodded. "I think it might work, he doesn't have any reason to be suspicious."

"As long as I can act like everything is fine," Jenny said with a sigh. At Charlie's inquisitive look, she grinned and patted his arm. "Don't worry Dad, I got this."

"You got this," he repeated while returning her grin. He shook his head. Kids. He glanced at Jimmy, who was now sitting next to Brooke and holding her hand again. He still looked groggy and was stoically watching and listening to what was happening.

He cast a bleary-eyed look at Charlie. "Don't know how much use I can be, but if you need me, I'm your man."

Charlie chuckled and shook his head. "Thanks, I think if you can watch over Brooke for us that will be a big help."

"No prob," Jimmy replied with a lopsided grin.

Charlie turned to his daughter, and then pointed. "I'm going to duck down by those boxes right next to the plastic partition. When he heads this way, grab Jake and both of you follow him, but stay back far enough that

308

he doesn't see you. Soon as he comes out, run up here and I'll grab him from behind, then you two can help me get him down."

Jenny glanced down at Malcolm, who was still glaring at them. "We should probably move him to the front so he can't be seen."

"Good idea."

She pointed at Brooke. "Should we move her, too?"

Charlie thought for a moment before shaking his head. "I think she's fine, even when we tussled with old Malcolm here we didn't get anywhere close to her and we're going to be several feet away."

With Jenny's help, they drug Malcolm to the front and sat him with his back against the side of a large metal desk. A tall bookcase on the other side obscured anyone's view of Malcolm if they were approaching from the rear of the tent.

"Perfect," Jenny remarked as Charlie grabbed a nearby cord and tied Malcolm to a desk leg. "Now he won't be able to wriggle around and cause a lot of noise."

Charlie straightened up. "Okay, let's get this Samuel guy up here before he comes on his own and catches us."

Jenny put a hand on his arm, her eyes big with concern. "Please be careful, this guy isn't Malcolm's bodyguard for no reason."

"Oh, don't worry, I'll be careful. Besides, I'm counting on you and Jake to help me out," Charlie said as they walked over to the plastic partition and he took his spot behind the boxes.

"Duck down, want to make sure no one can see you before I go back," Jenny said, worry evident in her voice.

Charlie dutifully hunkered down. "Can you see me?"

"Nope, not at all. Just be sure he is completely past you before you go after him, okay?"

"I got this," Charlie said with a wink and a grin as he stood up.

Jenny's eyes narrowed for a moment before she grinned back. "Cute." She sighed loudly and squared her shoulders. "Okay, here I go, wish me luck."

"Good luck," Charlie replied. "Don't worry, this will work."

"I hope for our sakes it does," his daughter retorted before disappearing on the other side of the partition.

As Charlie resumed his position behind the boxes, he hoped so, too. If things didn't go well, Beth and the others would have to find a way to get them out, and he didn't want them to put themselves in jeopardy. Heaven knew they had already been through enough.

He took a deep breath and tried to stay calm even though he could feel adrenalin begin to surge through his body. To his dismay, he could hear Jenny arguing with someone, most likely Samuel. Since he could hear her he knew they were almost to the partition. Back in the lab you couldn't hear any noises from up front due to all the hissing and whooshing coming from various tubes and lines feeding into Connor's chamber.

"Malcolm's not going to like this," Jenny said in a loud, angry voice. Charlie knew it was for his benefit and he decided to stay in place. Maybe they could somehow still pull this off; he would have to see once they came out.

He heard the rustle of plastic and froze. He could almost feel them step through and pause. Fear mixed with adrenaline and he began to sweat. He was afraid to

311

confront the bodyguard, but even more fearful not to – the last thing he wanted was to be under a furious Malcolm's thumb again.

"Where are they?"

"Not sure," Jenny said with a light, but slightly shaky chuckle. She moved past the boxes. "Looks like they probably went outside."

Charlie could barely make out the top of Samuel's head as he followed Jenny and moved beyond the boxes. He tensed and forced himself to wait.

"Maybe," the man grumbled. He gave Jenny a nudge forward. "Let's go check."

Charlie peeked around the corner of the boxes just in time to see Jenny fake a stumble and fall to her knees. As Samuel bent down to help her up, she chanced a quick glance at Charlie, signaling with her eyes.

Without another thought, Charlie stood and launched himself forward.

★★★★

He sat in the dark. For the moment, all was quiet inside his head and he liked the respite. The others were in a type of food-induced stupor. During the day they tended to retreat and lapse into a trance-like state. At night, they stirred and began to interact, sending images back and forth. They never slept. The stronger ones, like himself, could transmit emotions based on needs and a few commands.

He didn't realize it, but he was the strongest of them all. For a time, he didn't realize what he was able to do, but comprehension was slowly dawning. Only he could command complete obedience and call others to him. As he rested, he felt stronger by the moment and decided that perhaps it was time to reach out. He knew what to look for and when he connected with one of his kind, he quickly scanned the mind. If he liked what he found, he didn't command, but invited them to come.

He actually felt a little surprise at how many were out there. Before sunrise their numbers would once again grow quickly as most of those he touched decided to join him without any coercion on his part.

This is going to be easy, he thought to himself and for the first time in a long time, the corners of his rotting mouth turned upward into a ghastly and gruesome smile.

Chapter 25

Mick poured water into a rag he kept in his bag then rubbed it all over his face, wiping off some of the dirt and sweat in the process. He was grateful that they were all still in one piece and more importantly, still alive.

When Sean and Scott went around the front of the funeral home to find a way in, they literally ran into a huge swarm of zombies. They seemed to know there was a large concentration of people by the funeral home because Dexter later told them the zombies suddenly lost interest in the apartments and headed straight their way.

Mick and the others spent the next two hours alternating between fighting and retreating. They ended up at the high school where they now sat licking their wounds. He could still hear fierce fighting coming from the downtown area.

He had no idea how many people they lost on the way. Nelson and his men were still trying to make their way to the school. Judith was still with them, but Casey, Megan, and Darrell were nowhere to be found and not answering their walkies.

In the midst of the confusion and chaos, he almost lost track of Cindy and his sons, but they managed to stay together with the help of Captain Sears and his men.

The situation was bleak everywhere. Cindy managed to contact Dexter and he told them that after they retreated, zombies once again swarmed the apartments and this time they broke through. As a last resort he blew the stairs and now they were trapped on the upper floor and roof. They did have the ladders and when it was clear they would be able to get down, but for now they weren't going anywhere.

For the moment, Mick felt relatively safe enough to catch his breath. They sat lined up in the main hall of the school, backs against the lockers. He could tell Cindy was exhausted by the way she leaned against him.

He wondered what time it was, he lost his watch during the fighting. Later, what happened to them that night would be known as the Midnight Massacre, another sad chapter in the history of Shady Oaks. For now though, it felt as though hours had passed since he left Brooke back at the camp.

He was still feeling unbelievably guilty about not

telling Cindy and he glanced over at her, unease in his eyes. As though she felt his gaze, she turned her eyes up to him and gave him a weary smile. He returned the smile and hugged her to him. She rested her head on his shoulder with a tired sigh.

He smiled to himself when he heard Cindy's breathing deepen and become regular with sleep and as he listened, he felt his eyes grow heavy. Despite his resolve to stay awake, he dozed off, his head coming to rest atop his wife's.

He came awake with a start. Sean had him by one shoulder and was gently shaking him.

"What is it?" he managed to croak out. He cleared his throat and sat up, careful not to disturb Cindy.

"We heard from Nelson," Sean whispered as he sat on his haunches. "His men were scattered and they took heavy casualties. Those that are left are headed this way. When they get here, we're going to regroup and figure out what to do next."

"What does Sears say?" Mick asked with a yawn.

"He says to get everyone ready to go, he's not sure how long we'll be safe here. He's even thinking we may need to leave town and head back up the mountain for now."

That brought Mick fully awake. The situation must be even worse than he thought. "Give up Shady Oaks? We can't do that, especially after so many fought so hard."

Sean held up a hand. "Hang on there! No one said anything about giving up. He thinks it might be a good idea to go back because it will give us a safe place to formulate a good plan of attack. Everyone will get a chance to rest and get something to eat before heading back down, too."

Mick nodded, he could see the logic in that plan. "So, what else is he thinking?"

"Well, Nelson wants to stay and fight, see it through to the end. There's a lot of his men as well as some of ours who would like to continue on."

Mick stood and walked over to the nearest window to peer out. "The fog seems to be clearing, if we are going to head back up the mountain now might be the best time."

Sean joined him. "You're probably right; I'll go check to

317

see what's been decided, if anything."

Mick watched his son walk away and sighed heavily. He glanced back out the window. He really couldn't see much, it was still too dark and foggy. The fog would provide them with cover if they needed to move out, if it was lifting he knew there was a full moon and they would have a lot of trouble staying undetected. He was glad staying or going was one decision he didn't have to make.

Within moments, Sean exited a room down the hall and headed his way. "Looks like we're going," he said when he reached his father's side.

Mick nodded without replying. Father and son stood together silently, both gazing out the window without really looking at what was beyond the glass.

"We're really in a pickle, aren't we?" Mick said at last.

"Yeah," Sean responded softly. "When Scott and I first came to help out at Shady Oaks, the zombies were kinda spread out in groups and easily taken care of. Now they seem to be smarter and with a huge mass of them swarming us at every turn we can't get the upper hand. We need to get out of

318

here so we can formulate a winnable plan."

"Or we need a miracle," said a voice behind them. Mick turned and Cindy, wide awake, grabbed him by the hand.

"Or that," Sean said with a grim smile. "A miracle would do, that's for sure."

****

Charlie slammed so hard into Samuel's back that it almost knocked the breath out of him. Samuel stumbled over Jenny, who was still on her knees in front of him, and he went flying. Charlie struggled to hang on and wrapped his arms around the other man's chest in an effort to pin his arms at his sides. The bodyguard hit the floor head first so hard it knocked him out. Charlie lay atop him for a moment, breathing heavily. He couldn't believe their good luck. He turned to look at Jenny.

"You all right?" he managed to gasp out. She was getting up and dusting herself off.

"I think so, that was crazy," she remarked.

"That was lucky," he replied as he slowly eased himself off the inert man. "Go get Jake while I tie this guy up, okay?"

Jenny nodded and Charlie fished around in his back pocket for the cord he tucked in there earlier. As he began to work, Jenny returned with Jake at her side.

Jake's eyes widened. "What in the world have you two been doing while I've been busy?"

"Oh, just taking out the bad guys," Charlie said with a weak laugh as he bound the still unconscious man's hands together. "Malcolm's over there," he said with a nod.

Jake's mouth fell open. "You're not kidding, are you?" He walked over to see Malcolm strapped to the other side of the desk. He chuckled and shook his head.

"A little help here?" Charlie asked. Both Jenny and Jake rushed over and together they drug Samuel over by Malcolm and using more duct tape, secured him to the other side of the desk.

Charlie stood. "I'm going to grab Beth and the others, be right back."

Within moments the tent was full of people all trying to talk at once. Charlie smiled to himself and stepped outside, he wanted to take a minute while he had one to give Mick a call.

He was surprised when his friend responded almost immediately.

"Charlie, I'm glad to hear from you so soon," Mick said. "So how is it going?"

"We managed to get Malcolm and his bodyguard, everyone is fine. Brooke is still sleeping, Jimmy is with her, and Jake says we should have her results by dawn."

"Good to hear, I've really been worried," came the reply.

"I'm surprised I was able to reach you so easily, I figured you'd be in the thick of it by now."

Charlie heard the end of a dry laugh before Mick replied. "Well, we were in the thick of it, we were overrun and had to hoof it over to the high school. They're debating now what to do, some want to come back up the mountain to regroup and do some more planning."

Charlie was surprised. "I know there were a lot of zombies in that building, but with all the manpower down there, they should have been easily taken care of."

"I saw the zombies up there, too and you're right, I think we could have taken care of them. What you didn't see is about twice that number ended up here, I think they actually attracted more zombies on their way down. We're guessing there could be as many as four hundred in town right now."

Mick whistled softly, the most they ever dealt with was under half that. "Why don't you let me know what the final decision is, we can either come down there to help or get things ready if everyone comes back here."

Even though Charlie couldn't see him, Mick nodded. "Will do. While we're both waiting, I'm thinking that it's time to tell Cindy what happened to Brooke."

"Don't worry, Cindy's not the type to place blame on something like that."

Mick sighed. "I know, but I still hate having to tell her, knowing how upset she will be. She'll want to head straight up there and I'm not sure that's such a good idea just yet."

"Well, like I said, keep us posted," Charlie said. "Talk to you soon."

"Copy that."

Mick turned and saw Cindy standing right next to him. By the quizzical look on her face, he knew she heard at least some of the conversation.

He glanced around the hall, everything was quiet for the

moment, which meant now was as good a time as any to come clean.

"Were you saying something about Brooke?"

Mick sighed again and took her by the arm, leading her toward an empty room. "Come with me, I need to tell you something."

★★★★

Charlie took a few minutes to pass on everything Mick told him. Then he turned to Jake.

"I'm thinking we need to do some rearranging. Why don't we keep Brooke and Jimmy here and move everyone else over to the other big tent? We can move those hospital beds over here and we can move Brooke to one instead of that tiny cot she's on now.

"Probably a good idea," Jake replied. He grasped Charlie by the elbow and leaned in. "Listen," he said in a low voice. "Is there anyone in Beth's group who would be up to disposing of those nasty zombies in the crates before anyone else goes in there?"

"I'll ask," Charlie said. "Let me go talk to them about what we're planning and see if someone will volunteer to put them out of their misery, then put them out in the field with the others."

Soon everyone was busy with a task. Hunter and his father took Malcolm and Samuel and put them in the holding cell in the office building. The rest busied themselves with getting furniture moved around and Jake oversaw moving Brooke to one of the hospital beds as soon as it was set up. She stirred and moaned, but didn't wake.

After checking her vitals, Jake gave a satisfied nod and disappeared behind the plastic partition. Charlie assumed he was checking the tests. Once again, Charlie found himself saying a silent prayer that they would be able to give Brooke the vaccine and she would be all right.

He went to the other tent and found an older man and his son who agreed to dispose of the crated zombies. While they were at their grisly task, he walked out to survey the field. The fog was lifting and it was easier to see what needed done.

He went back to the main tent and soon returned with one of Malcolm's flatbed trucks. There was no way they could leave all the contaminated bodies near the lake. From previous experience, he knew they needed to be moved, burned, and buried.

He removed his jacket and rolled up his sleeves. After donning a pair of gloves he found in a large tool box behind the cab, he started dragging bodies over.

When Beth, Hunter, and several others approached he heaved a sigh of relief. They were all wearing gloves, some carried shovels, and a few were now armed with rifles. Beth set a lantern on the bed of the truck and smiled at him.

"We finished moving everything around and Hunter saw you out here. Figured you needed some help."

"I sure do, you have perfect timing," he said as he returned the smile.

As they were finishing up, the two crated zombies, now headless, were added to the pile in the truck. After a quick discussion, it was decided to take them down the hill away from any water source. Hunter volunteered to handle the burning and burial and Charlie happily agreed, he had other things that needed his attention. As he watched them load up and drive away, Jenny joined him.

"Will the day ever come when we don't have to do that anymore?"

Charlie sighed and put an arm around her shoulders. "I think so. Maybe after we get Shady Oaks cleaned up again we'll be done with all this, especially if we have a vaccine for this thing."

"That's what everyone is hoping for. Jake wanted me to tell you that the next time you talk to Mick or anyone in town, be sure to tell them if someone is scratched or bitten to isolate and secure them until we can get them up here to see if they can be treated."

"Good idea, we can probably save a lot of people," Charlie replied. "One other thing, remind me tomorrow morning to have a few men sweep this field to make sure we didn't miss any creepy crawlies."

"Got it," Jenny said. She turned and gestured toward the tent. "I'm going back, are you coming?"

"I'll be there in a few, think I'll see if I can get Mick on the walkie and see what they've decided. That way I can come in and let everyone know what's going on."

To his surprise, Sean was the one who responded, telling Charlie that Mick gave him his walkie before going off with Cindy to explain what happened to Brooke.

"I see," he replied. He was glad he wasn't in Mick's shoes at the moment. "We've been busy up here getting things ready in case everyone heads this way, do you know if anything's been decided yet?"

"As a matter of fact, now I'm hearing we are staying put for now. There's a plan in the works, but haven't heard what it is yet."

"All right, let your dad know we talked, okay? Oh, and one other thing, pass the word along if anyone is scratched or bitten they need to be isolated then brought up here so they can be tested to see if the vaccine will work for them. We don't need anyone dying needlessly because they think there's nothing that can be done."

"Good thinking, will pass it on. Talk to you soon."

"Copy that," Charlie responded. He looked toward the tents as he clipped the walkie back into place. Now that they had the situation fairly well under control he felt the urge to head down to Shady Oaks. He hated the idea that his friends were in danger and he couldn't do anything to help them other than offer a little advice.

He saw a figure emerge, switch on a flashlight, and head his way. Jake gave him a grin as he lowered his light and came to stand beside him. "Jenny told me you were still out here; I'd like to ask you something."

"Ask away," he responded amicably. The more he was around Jake; the more he liked the young doctor.

"I've been talking to the doctors and scientists who've been working for Malcolm. I don't agree with what Malcolm had them do, but what you and I would consider the really bad ones, they were weeded out awhile ago. These men that are left are dedicated to finding a vaccine that everyone can benefit from. I'd like to keep working up here if possible and I need their help."

Charlie stood for a moment looking up at the sky, where a few tentative stars seemed to be dodging in and out of the clearing fog. He glanced at Jake.

"I can't promise you anything, Jake. Whether directly responsible or not, a lot of people were hurt or lost their lives. When the time comes we'll have to decide what to do with them on an individual basis, but I would say that their dedication puts them in a somewhat favorable light."

At Jake's crestfallen look, he said, "I'll pass on what you've said to the captain and the others, I'm sure they will be interested in what you have to say."

"Guess that's about the best I can ask for right now," Jake said reluctantly. "Please emphasize though that I need these men and their research."

"I understand how important they are and will pass that along."

"So, have you heard from Mick yet?"

"As a matter of fact, I just finished talking to Sean. Let's head back inside and I'll pass on what he told me."

He noticed headlights coming up the dirt road, bouncing up and down and skimming the tree line. Hunter was back sooner than expected and met them at the entrance to the tent.

"We found a good spot and it's going to take a good while for all those bodies to burn," he said as he nodded toward the southeast. Charlie followed his gaze and made out a faint red glow through the trees. "A couple guys stayed behind to watch the fire. We're planning to go back sometime tomorrow to bury the remains."

"You mean sometime today, it's past midnight," Charlie said. "Let me know when. I'm thinking it would be nice if I can manage to get the captain to let one of his chaplains come up here to go with you to say a few words."

Hunter nodded. "Good idea, maybe we could even have a little service of some kind."

Charlie nodded and gestured with his flashlight toward the tent. "After you."

A sudden wave of fatigue washed over him. Coffee was definitely needed before he did anything else. He followed the others inside and made a beeline straight for the kitchenette, which was directly on the other side of the plastic divider. He sighed with happiness when he saw a full pot in the coffeemaker.

Jenny was standing nearby talking to Beth and she glanced at him and smiled. He smiled back and pointed.

"Coffee. Need some. Now please."

The two women chuckled as they watched him scurry over and grab a paper cup, quickly filling it with steaming coffee. He began to blow then sip the hot liquid, grimacing as it burned his tongue, but it had the desired effect. He could feel the heat course through him and it helped chase away the fatigue.

"I guess Jake talked to you?" Jenny asked. She gave him a questioning look.

He nodded and took another sip. Ah, heaven in a cup he thought. He looked at his daughter. "We talked and I told him I would pass on his request, but I'm in no position to make any decision, especially right now."

"Understood," Jenny remarked.

"By the way, I heard from Sean and I need to get everyone together, let them know what's going on in Shady Oaks. Why don't we head back to the main room?"

As he turned to go, he heard his walkie crackle to life and after a moment, Mick's voice came through. As he pulled it free, he held up a hand. "Would you mind going on and getting everyone together while I take this?"

"Sure thing," Jenny said. She stopped and gave him a quick kiss on the cheek before stepping through the plastic.

He hadn't expected to hear from Mick so soon and frowned. Sometimes no news was good news and with Mick calling him back so soon, it made him nervous.

He took a deep breath and pushed the button. "Charlie here."

****

He still sat with his back against the cold and damp stone wall of the basement. He thought there was more than enough room for them, but he was wrong. So many came, and many more were on their way. By daylight the building would be unable to hold any more, which meant they would be milling around outside where they could easily be seen.

Instinctively, he knew they had to move, if they were discovered now they would surely be destroyed. He really wanted to stay put, he was satiated from feeding and his distended stomach made it difficult to move. With a groan, he placed a mottled and gore-covered hand against the wall and slowly pulled himself up.

Those around him began to stir as he filled their empty minds with an imagine of them moving as a group down the smaller dirt side road that led off into the thick stand of trees that lined the base of the mountain. As they stood, he turned and made his way slowly up the stairs.

Those waiting on the first floor made way for him and fell into line behind him as he passed by. He wasn't sure where to go, he only knew they needed to go the opposite direction from where they recently fed. He stepped outside and slowly shambled toward the dirt road.

Chapter 26

Cindy wiped her eyes again and sniffed. Mick watched her with concern. She was taking what he told her better than expected. She hadn't even said anything about him leaving Brooke at the camp.

She looked at him with red-rimmed eyes. "I knew eventually something would happen to one of us, the odds weren't in our favor to stay fairly unscathed by all this."

He rubbed her back silently as she continued. "I knew I should have made her stay here, I was uneasy about her going, we didn't even know what it was like up there. I feel like this is all my fault."

Mick tilted his head to look at her, surprised. "If anyone has anything to feel guilty about, it's me. I was supposed to watch out for her. Not only did she get hurt, but then I left her up there."

Cindy shook her head. "I guess we are both going to feel guilty no matter what, but the hard truth is we can't protect them from everything. Besides, she's in the best hands possible right now and she'd only be in more danger down here."

335

"True. Hadn't thought about it that way," Mick admitted. He heard voices coming from down the hall and looked up. "Sounds like something's going on, let's go check it out."

Cindy gave him a faint smile. "All right, just promise me that as soon as this is over we'll head up to be with Brooke."

"Promise," he said solemnly before heading for the door. He almost ran into Scott at the threshold.

"C'mon you two, Nelson made it here with his men and he's got Dexter with him!"

Mick raised an eyebrow and taking Cindy's hand, followed his son down the hall. As they approached the thick glass doors that led outside, he saw a large group of people standing around.

As they exited the building and went down the short flight of steps, Cindy pointed and leaned toward him. "There's Dexter," she said loudly in his ear so she could be heard, it seemed to Mick that everyone was trying to talk at once.

Mick squinted, then nodded. A slight but steady breeze was blowing away what was left of the fog, and the nearly full moon was high in the sky, illuminating everything in a pale, cold light.

Scott stopped abruptly and Mick saw Captain Sears approaching, with Nelson and Dexter on his heels. They bounded up the steps and turning, the captain held up a hand.

"Can I get everyone's attention, please?" Instant silence greeted him and he smiled. "Thank you. After much discussion, I wanted to explain what's going on. Nelson here tells me he believes we can defeat these things and that there's no reason to put it off. Mr. Reed," he said with a gesture toward Dexter, "Informs me that his men up on the apartment roof were beginning to make a rather large dent in the numbers as they picked them off one by one."

He looked around at the men and women standing before him. "We need to decide if we want to stay and fight, or should we head back up to the camp where we can regroup and do some planning."

"If we let those things run around willy nilly while we're lounging around at this camp, they're going to do even more damage. We've worked too hard to get this town up and running again to just hand it over," a dark-haired woman Mick knew only as Milly said. "And what about the people in the shelter? They would be stuck in there until we returned."

There were several murmurs of agreement, and Mick knew right then what the final decision would be. In the end, it was unanimous that they would stay and fight. After another hurried discussion, Nelson gathered up his men and disappeared into the night.

To Mick's dismay, Dexter was put in charge of all civilians and he immediately began to bellow orders in true Dexter style. The last thing Mick wanted to do was fight his way through zombies again. Fortunately, Cindy, Judith, and a few others were to stay at the school and keep a watch on the roof and take out any stray zombies who headed their way.

Mick wasn't the least bit surprised that Sean and Scott were going with Sears and after a few quick hugs and reassurances, they hurried off.

He turned to Cindy and wrapped his arms around her. He rested his chin on the top of her head and held her tight. He was afraid to leave her alone, although he knew that other than the shelter, she would be safe up on the school roof away from the reach of any zombie. He held her until he felt a large and heavy hand fall on his shoulder.

"Time to go," Dexter growled.

Cindy looked up as Mick released her. "Have you heard from Darrel, Megan, Casey, or Rose?"

"Haven't heard from anyone other than Rose, I talked to her when I was stuck on the roof. I was able to reach her on the walkie when I saw some of the people from the shelter come up when the church bells rang. Told her to get them back inside. I saw her come up and talk to a few of them before Nelson's men showed up. She ran back in when they started rounding people up."

"Oh, I'm glad she didn't get caught," Cindy remarked.

"She was back inside the shelter with Kevin when the zombies made their way down there," Dexter said. He grunted as he shifted his backpack from one shoulder to another. "She said they had to fight them off to get the door closed and some people didn't make it."

Cindy gasped and Mick put an arm around her shoulders. "What! How in the world did zombies end up down there?" he asked in dismay.

Dexter shrugged. "No idea, maybe they were attracted to the commotion Nelson's men were making when they were taking themselves some prisoners and found an open door. By the way, what's up with all these naked and bald zombies – and some have what looks like medical scrubs or paper gowns on?"

Mick shook his head. "We have Malcolm, the leader of the Connor Group to thank for that, but I'll explain more later when we have more time."

Dexter looked at his watch. "Speaking of time, we really gotta go. Are you ready?"

Mick sighed. "Ready as I'll ever be, I suppose."

He turned to Cindy as Judith walked up and linked an arm through her's. "Take care of her for me," he said to Judith and gave her a small smile.

She smiled back. "Don't worry, she can take care of herself, but I'll be there if she does need me."

Cindy blew him a kiss as Judith began to drag her away by the arm. "See you soon!"

"I'll call you on the walkie when it's all clear," Mick said with a small wave.

Dexter grunted again and gave Mick a nudge. "C'mon man, we don't have all day; everyone else is in place and ready to move."

Mick hesitated. "Go on ahead; I'll be there in a few."

Dexter gave him a quizzical look, but for once didn't push the issue and ambled off.

He wanted to let Charlie know what was going on so they could start preparing. With what they were up against, Mick was certain they were going to have several more injured on their hands. He quickly keyed the mike.

★★★★

"Charlie here, what's up Mick?"

"Sean filled me in on what you two discussed," came the reply. "He passed the info on and I wanted to let you know we're about to go finish this, one way or the other."

Charlie frowned. "Wish I could be there."

He heard Mick give a wry chuckle. "No you don't. Trust me. I wanted to give you a heads up so you have time to get ready for the injured we'll be bringing up."

"From what I've seen, I think we have everything we need."

"Sounds good, but if you haven't already, you might want to set up a quarantine area. We know there will be some who won't be able to tolerate the vaccine and we'll need a place to put them."

Charlie gave himself a mental slap upside the head. "Good idea, I knew there was something we were forgetting!"

"I'm hoping we get lucky, but we both know not everyone will make it," said Mick with such sadness in his voice that it carried over the walkie.

"Well, let's stay optimistic then," Charlie said with forced reassurance.

"How is Brooke, is she still sleeping?"

"Like a baby," Charlie said as he glanced toward the tent.

"Any news from Jake yet?"

"Not yet, but could be anytime now."

"All right, guess I should get going. No matter what though, the minute you know anything give me a shout, okay?"

"You got it. How is Judith?"

"She's with Cindy and they are safe and sound up on the high school roof."

"That's a relief," Charlie responded.

"Dexter's glaring at me and heading this way so guess I'd better go," Mick said with a sigh.

"All right, take care of yourself," Charlie said as sudden tears stung his eyes. He felt a deep and surprising fear. He tried to swallow, gulping past the large lump in his throat.

He heard a chuckle. "I'm always careful," Mick replied.

"You'd better be," Charlie said. "If you haven't heard from me by the time you're finished down there, give me a call."

"Will do, signing off for now."

Charlie stared at the walkie in his hand for what seemed like minutes. At that moment, he didn't know what to say, do, or think. His friends and the place he'd come to know as home was in mortal danger and all he could do was stand there. He looked up into the now clear sky. The moon shone brightly, illuminating everything around him, for which he was thankful.

From the corner of his eye, he saw someone emerge from the tent and as they approached he was surprised to see it was Jake. He was waving what looked like a large folder.

He skid to a stop in front of Charlie and waved the folder under his nose. "I didn't realize this, but before they had to leave Connor's blood was already being tested and we just got the results."

Charlie raised an eyebrow. "Really? So what does it tell us?"

"Well, it tells us we need to talk to Malcolm," Jake replied.

"So I'm guessing the vaccine will work for Connor," Charlie said with a growing excitement. If it worked for Connor, he couldn't help but hope it would work for Brooke and the others.

Jake smacked him on the arm with the folder. "You got it! Now we need to talk to Malcolm. We know what he will say, but he's still Connor's father and I guess it's kind of ingrained in me that we should get his permission to go ahead with treatment."

Charlie nodded. "Lead the way."

As they approached, a man sitting by the front door stood

up. Charlie recognized him as Hunter's father. He was holding a shotgun in both hands and silently eyed them up and down.

Jake nodded toward the door. "We need to talk to Malcolm."

Without a word, he turned the knob and opened the door for them. Once inside, Jake turned to Charlie and grinned.

"Guess he's a man of few words."

"I'll say," Charlie said as he grinned back. He looked over Jake's shoulder where he could see into the next room. Another man, one he didn't recognize, sat in a chair watching their two prisoners. His hands rested on a rifle lying across his lap.

As they entered the room, the man gave them a nod, stood up, and offered a hand to first Jake and then Charlie.

"I'm Jose Gonzales and I'd like to thank you for saving my wife and me," he said with a wide smile as he vigorously shook their hands.

"Glad we could help," Jake said quickly. He glanced at the men in the cell. "We'd like a few minutes with Malcolm, please. Would you like to take a break while we're here?"

"Sure thing, thank you," Jose replied. He turned, then hesitated. "Here," he said as he handed Charlie the rifle. "You might want to keep this, just in case."

As the man hurried out, Charlie leaned against the wall as Jake grabbed the chair and pulled it closer to the cell where Malcolm and Samuel sat staring at them.

"Well, what did we do to deserve the pleasure of your company?" Malcolm asked with a sneer.

"We're not here to play games with you," Jake said, ignoring the taunt. "I've got some news about Connor."

Immediately, Malcolm stood up and strode over to the cell door, grabbing a bar in each hand. Charlie tightened his grip on the rifle.

Jake held up a hand. "Calm down, Malcolm. We got the results back and the news is good. Connor should tolerate the vaccine with no problem."

Malcolm visibly relaxed and let out a big breath, then his eyes narrowed. "Should? You haven't given him the vaccine yet? What are you waiting for?"

"Why, your permission of course," Jake said casually. "Even though you're a cold-blooded murderer, you're still his father and I felt we still needed your go-ahead to treat him."

Malcolm shook his head. "Of course you have my permission, but I do have one request."

"What would that be?"

"I want to be there when he wakes up."

Jake gave Charlie a quick glance and he shrugged with a slight shake of his head.

"That's a decision that has to be discussed with the others first," Charlie said to Jake, pointedly ignoring Malcolm.

"Once he's given the vaccine, it will be awhile before we even attempt to wake him and then it will be a very slow process," Jake added as he glanced back at Malcolm. "He's been down for a long time and we have to be very careful."

Malcolm glared at the young doctor. "If anything happens to my son..."

Jake stood up, frowning. "Your threats mean nothing to me. Not everyone is a heartless bastard like you." As Jake turned on his heel and strode out, Charlie walked closer to Malcolm.

"You're the worst kind of stupid, aren't you?" he spat out in disgust. "Jake will take care of Connor like he was his own son and he will even ask that you be present when he wakes up, which is way more than you deserve."

He turned without waiting for a reply and after returning the rifle to Jose, hurried to catch up with Jake, who was still silently fuming. Charlie placed a hand on his shoulder as they walked. "Don't let him get to you, try to stay focused on what you're doing, which is saving a lot of lives."

Jake glanced at him before nodding. "I can't help wondering how men like that are able to not only survive, but thrive without someone taking them out. Malcolm seems to have the ability to take normally decent, good people and turn them into versions of himself."

"Makes me wonder what kind of person Connor is," Charlie commented.

Jake slowed his pace. "Well, the truth is, we may never find that out. Malcolm knows as well as I do that there's a good chance Connor may never wake up."

"If he doesn't wake up, we'd better make sure we keep Malcolm under a tight reign, no telling what he'd do," Charlie muttered. He didn't like the idea of a raging Malcolm getting loose to exact his type of sadistic and brutal revenge.

As they neared the entrance to the tent, Jake stopped. "I'm going to go administer the vaccine to Connor. I'll keep you posted on his condition."

Charlie nodded and as he followed Jake inside, he prayed that all would go well. His thoughts drifted to Mick and the others, and he said another prayer for them, too. They could use all the help they could get.

★★★★

He stood on a ridge that overlooked what could be called a small village. Haverton was fortunate, they acted quickly and were able to keep the infection at bay. The perimeter was heavily patrolled and all entry points protected by at least two guards.

None of this mattered to him or his horde. He was only waiting for his stragglers and for the sun to set behind the mountain, then they would proceed down the ridge and take what they wanted.

Several towns and small farms lined the base of Fletcher Mountain, they would prove fairly easy to invade and overcome.

Each conquest would make them stronger and at the same time provide more followers. They were already a formidable army of the undead and they were about to get even stronger. He gave the mental signal to move forward and as one, they silently took their first step off the ridge.

Chapter 27

"So what are we supposed to do?" Mick asked as he trudged along at Dexter's side.

"Since we don't have the same level of training as the others, we lag back and catch any strays that get by."

Dexter's group was waiting quietly and as they approached, Dexter began shouting orders again. He pointed across the street at the apartment building where most of the zombies were currently swarming.

Mick could see several dark figures of men on the roof. They were running back and forth, yelling and whooping to keep the zombies' attention on them so the men on the ground could sneak up from behind.

They were picking the zombies off with carefully placed shots, but stopped with all the men below them. The possibility of accidentally shooting one of their own was too great a chance to take.

In the waning fog, Mick made out the line of uniformed men slowly moving forward. He squinted, hoping to see Sean or Scott, but it was too dark. He didn't know where Nelson and his men were, but he assumed they were probably coming in from either side. He knew the idea was to box the zombies in, pushing them toward the apartment building where there would be no escape.

"We stay twenty paces back," Dexter told the men and women standing before him. "If any of those things get by the men in front of us, it's our job to take them out. Don't shoot unless you have a clear target, we don't need any deadly mistakes. Most of you have other weapons like axes or machetes; try to use them if you can."

For emphasis, Dexter pulled out a large knife and flashed it above his head. "I used this bad boy on a zombie and took him right out."

Mick shuddered, he though he heard Dexter proudly tell the story many times. "If you can, take the head clean off, at the very least try to stick 'em in the eye to get at the brain."

A loud whistle got their attention. "All right ladies and gents, that's our signal to look sharp. Here we go."

Mick glanced down at the knife holstered on his hip as he

swung the rifle he was handed earlier off his shoulder. He wasn't certain he could drive a blade into a person's eye, even if they were technically dead.

As the line of soldiers began to advance with Dexter's group following, the zombies soon came into view, and the ensuing barrage of gunfire was frightening as well as deafening.

Breaking into a cold sweat, he tightened his hold on the rifle as he raised it into position and moved slowly forward.

The idea was to literally mow down the zombies with massive firepower. That plan almost immediately went out the window. The whole mass turned as one and surged forward when the soldiers opened fire. As zombies fell, the ones behind them continued on and within moments everyone was in slow retreat, but still shooting steadily.

Mick felt the beginnings of panic start to overtake him and to his relief; he spotted first Scott and then Sean coming his way at a quick jog. Within seconds, they flanked him.

"Come with us!" Scott yelled in his ear. Mick nodded and they began to move back toward the street at a faster pace. He noticed that both of them now had M9 bayonets, or multipurpose knives, attached to their M-16s in case of close quarter fighting. He carried the same knife because of Sean's insistence that it was not just a weapon but an invaluable tool.

Both his sons raised their weapons and began firing as they continued to carefully move backward. From his peripheral vision he could see men scurrying back and forth as they fired on the swarm before them.

As he raised his own rifle, a strange sound came from behind the apartment building and for a brief moment, everyone paused. He squeezed his eyes shut when a beam of light temporary blinded him. He felt a strong wind wash over them and he looked up and pointed.

"It's Harry and Mark!" He shouted excitedly. As a zombie lurched toward him, Sean stabbed it in the head and drove it to the ground where he put a bullet right between the eyes for good measure. He looked up.

"Great timing," he said with a wink at Mick.

The Huey came down even lower, and the zombies flocked

toward it with arms upraised. They were fascinated with the noise and light, forgetting everything else around them.

Another light emanated from the chopper, illuminating the ground directly below. When they swung around, Mick was able to make out a figure, which he assumed was Mark, sitting on the floorboard. As zombies continued to flock toward the hovering Huey, Mark began to mow down zombies with the mounted .50 caliber machine gun.

On the ground, Captain Sears and Nelson's men quickly fell in together and began to inch forward in a line, slowly heading toward the zombies under the chopper. Mick was glad that Sean and Scott decided to stay by his side, with all the chaos and commotion he wasn't sure what to do.

Corporal Riley ran up to Sean, shouting something into his ear as he thrust a plastic bag into his hands. He spun around and jogged the other way, Mick watched him stop in front of Dexter and hand him another bag. Mick peered over Sean's shoulder as he opened the bag. Sean pulled out a handful of blue latex gloves and quickly handed a pair to Mick.

"The captain wants us to make sure any zombie down on the ground is dead and if not, we're to dispatch them. Then we need to drag them over and roll them into the ditch for the time being."

Mick nodded and as he fumbled with the gloves, watched the carnage occurring before him. Looking down, he shook his head as he finished getting on the gloves. He wondered if there would ever come a time when life would get back to some semblance of normalcy for any of them. There were times when it seemed as though they were getting a handle on their situation, then something like Malcolm's men or this massive zombie horde comes in and disrupts everything.

Scott nudged him in the ribs, for which Mick was grateful because he hated when he thoughts turned morose. His son handed him a large hook and Mick groaned inwardly.

Their group began to slowly move forward again. Whenever Mick came upon a zombie, he carefully checked for head wounds. If there were none, he quickly ran the blade of his knife through an eye or ear before hooking the corpse near the collar bone and dragging it quickly to the ditch where he jerked the hook free before rolling the body down to join the others.

No one talked, everyone focused on the grisly task before them. Beside, who could talk with all the shooting, moaning, and shouting going on at the same time. Not to mention the noise and wind from the chopper.

Despite it all, Mick managed to concentrate on the task before him. The dew-covered grass was slick and got worse as zombie blood, gore, and no telling what else covered the ground. Everyone was slipping and trying to walk carefully, which was difficult when dragging bodies across the yard.

He lost track of time and glanced up in surprise when Sean put a hand on his shoulder. He looked around, hook still in hand. Only a few zombies remained on the ground. The Huey slowly lifted off and headed in the direction of the soccer field. The sudden silence felt strange, for several seconds no one moved, they just stared quietly at one another.

Without a word people began to slowly move off, most heading back toward the school. Scott joined them and Mick found himself

357

once again between his sons as
they followed the main group back.

At that moment, all Mick
wanted was to have his family back
together, a hot shower, and his
bed...in that order. He knew that
all of those things were possible,
but more than likely still several
hours away from obtaining, so he
squared his shoulders. As he
passed the huge mound of reeking
bodies now overflowing from the
ditch, he yanked off his gloves
and almost angrily threw them on
top.

The first person he saw as
they neared the school was Cindy.
The fog was gone and illuminated
by the moonlight; she was standing
on her tiptoes obviously watching
for them. They locked eyes and she
waved furiously. She gave Judith a
nudge and nodded in their
direction. Judith turned to look
and she smiled. Cindy grabbed her
by the arm and together they
jogged over.

She wrapped her arms around
Mick's neck and hugged him hard.
Reaching out with one hand, then
the other, she grabbed each twin
and pulled them into a family hug.
The four of them stood together
silently, before someone clearing
their throat interrupted the
moment. Mick looked over Cindy's

head to see Dexter standing next to Judith.

"Sorry to break up your little family reunion, but we still have some business to attend to," Dexter said grimly.

"We're going to touch base with Sarah and Denise, then see if there's anything we can help with," Sean said with a wave of his hand. Mick watched them walk off then turned to Dexter.

In characteristic Dexter style, he puffed out his chest before speaking again. "I need you and Cindy to go with Judith and start getting the injured people together. The captain wants anyone bitten or scratched moved up to the camp. He said if you can help with that, he'll see to it that you and Cindy go with the first group so you can be with Brooke as soon as possible."

Mick glanced at Cindy and Judith; they both gave him a nod. He looked at Dexter. "Absolutely, just point us in the right direction and we'll get right on that."

Dexter pointed toward the other end of the parking lot. "Go all the way down, there are people down there already setting up some kind of triage. I'm heading down to get everyone out of the shelter, when they're all moved I'll come help."

He turned to go, then paused and turned back. "Speaking of Brooke, I'm sorry about what happened and I'm keeping my fingers crossed for her."

Before Mick could reply, Dexter turned on his heel and hurried off.

"Well, that was nice," Cindy said, clearly surprised.

"Sure was," Mick agreed. "Sometimes Dexter can be full of surprises."

Cindy had one arm linked through Mick's and she linked the other through Judith's. "Shall we get going?"

As they walked, she glanced up at Mick. "Sounded like things got kind of bad over there, I'm so glad Harry and Mark made it, we could hear the chopper over here."

Mick paused. "Yeah, it was bad and they pretty much saved the day."

Judith grinned. "Cindy had the foresight to call them up on the walkie. They wanted to drive back earlier, but she asked them to wait just in case. Sure enough, the fog lifted and they were able to come in and help."

As they approached, a figure stood and waved. "Who is that?" Mick asked, squinting.

"Not sure - oh, it's Megan!" Judith said excitedly.

Megan trotted over to them and after giving Judith and Cindy a hug, she stepped back to look at them. "Darrell's been scratched," she said solemnly as she gestured toward a group of people huddled together. "We're waiting with the other wounded."

Mick winced. "We're here to help, and will be taking everyone up to the camp for treatment soon."

"That's what we heard," Megan replied as she turned to head back.

As they followed Megan, Cindy asked, "We lost track of Casey, is he here?"

Megan froze in mid-step for a moment before moving forward again with a shake of her head. "He didn't make it," she whispered loud enough for them to hear. She didn't turn to look at them. "I really don't want to talk about that right now, it was awful."

Cindy hurried over to put an arm around her friend. Judith bowed her head and gave Megan a pat on the back. Mick followed behind as the three friends murmured to each other, heads together as they walked. He was sick of people dying and hoped it was finally over.

He stopped when he heard the sound of a large vehicle approaching. As the military truck pulled up, he saw Sean in the driver's seat. The back gate swung down and Scott jumped from the back and approached them.

He was relieved to see them; he wanted to get Cindy up to Brooke as soon as possible. As another truck pulled up beside the first, Sean whistled to get everyone's attention.

"Let's get a move on, I want anyone who is badly injured or was scratched or bitten to have first priority, the next truck will take everyone with minor injuries."

After a quick hello and many reassurances to a nervous Darrell, Mick and the others helped get both trucks loaded.

"Let's go," Scott said as he offered a hand to help Judith get into the back of the truck. Once she was safely inside he turned to his parents. "Sean's already in back, you're with me," he said curtly as he slammed the gate shut.

Within moments they were on
their way up the rutted and bumpy
dirt road. Cindy sat between them
and feeling her gaze on him, Mick
turned and gave her what he hoped
was a confident smile as he put an
arm around her and gave her a
gentle squeeze. Finally they were
on their way, and he knew they
were all thinking of was getting
to Brooke as soon as possible. He
closed his eyes and forced himself
to relax, if he didn't he was
afraid he'd start blubbering like
a baby.

****

Brooke slowly opened her eyes
and yawned. Someone was holding
her hand, but she couldn't see who
it was. Everything was blurry; she
rubbed her eyes and yawned again
loudly.

She jumped when everyone
standing around her bed chuckled.
Cindy was holding her hand and
Mick stood by her head on the
other side. Next to him were Sean
and Scott. Jenny, Charlie, and
Jake stood together at the foot of
the bed. Jimmy was still resting
his back, but he was in the bed
next to her.

"What's going on?" she said, slurring the words slightly. She frowned and rubbed her eyes again as her memory started to return. She looked up, now everyone was slowly coming in to focus and she noticed the other beds full of patients. "Did I miss something?"

Mick glanced at his wife over Brooke's head, the relief he was feeling was mirrored in her eyes and they smiled at each other.

"A little, we'll fill you in later," Mick said as he gently ruffled her hair.

Although Jake was very busy, he took a few more moments to quickly check her vitals. Earlier, after administering the vaccine to Connor, he started the process of bringing him out of the coma and was pleased that the boy was responding quickly with no complications. Darrell's scratches turned out to be minor and Jake thought he'd be fine, but was still testing him to make sure if he needed the vaccine he could be treated.

Jake gave her a big smile. "You're going to be fine." He held up a finger. "As a matter of fact, you can go home as soon as you are up and able to move about on your own."

Brooke's eye grew big with happiness and she sat up. "I can't wait!" As she moved, she grimaced and looked down at her leg under the thin blanket. She looked up at Jake.

"That leg will be sore for a few days, keep it clean, take all the antibiotics, and you'll be running around again in no time."

Brooke nodded and as everyone began to disperse, Brooke asked for Jimmy. Cindy moved out of the way so Brooke could see. Jimmy, lying on his side, gave her a goofy grin and a wave. Megan and Darrell, with one arm securely wrapped in bandages, stood next to their son and were talking together in low voices.

"Can you move him closer to me so we can talk, please?" she asked her brothers.

They immediately took hold of Jimmy's bed and slid it closer. She grabbed his hand and as they began to share their experiences, Mick saw his chance to go outside. He wanted to check with Dexter, who was still in Shady Oaks, as to whether it would be safe to bring Brooke home later that afternoon. He grabbed Cindy's hand on the way out and gave her a gentle tug.

Smiling, she turned and went with him.

Exiting the tent, he paused and put an arm around her. The sun was rising, turning the sky from a murky purple to a deep blue. Although incredibly tired, he took a deep breath of the fresh, clean air and smiled.

Together, they had survived another day – and together as a family they would continue to fight if they had to. Saying a deeply felt prayer of thanks, he stepped out into the bright new day.

★★★★

His luck wouldn't last forever, but for now victory was within grasp. He would never know that he would become a legend, he would be given outlandish names by story tellers and a few would stick, such as the Zombie King, and Destroyer of Men. Every man, woman, and child around would know the stories and pass them on.

His horde would rampage, causing chaos and death, but only for a short time. The vaccine, quickly followed by a permanent cure, would severely impede on their success.

He would fight to the bitter end, but instead of going out in a blaze of glory, he and his zombie army would eventually fade away until seen no more.

That time was yet to come, however. Surrounded by his brethren, he turned hungry eyes toward another town. He seemed to smile, his mottled and rotting lips curled back to reveal broken and jagged teeth, with bits of stringy flesh caught between them and a few dangling down to his chin.

For now, the world was still his for the taking. With a slight nod, he gave a mental command and they surged onward.

THE END

For more information on my books please visit:

https://www.facebook.com/CharRobinson.Author?ref=profile#!/Author.CharRobinson

Or

http://char-thechatterbox.blogspot.com/

Made in the USA
Lexington, KY
06 March 2014